Proclivity

Bonnie L. Kern

PublishAmerica
Baltimore

First printing

All characters in this book are fictitious, and any resemblance to real persons, living or dead, is coincidental.

ISBN: 1-4241-7210-1
PUBLISHED BY PUBLISHAMERICA, LLLP
www.publishamerica.com
Baltimore

Printed in the United States of America

DEDICATION

This book is dedicated to my deceased daughter. We never got the opportunity to build a relationship. I hope she is proud of the person I have become.

It is dedicated to all of the women who are suffering from the aftereffects of being molested and abused as children.

It is dedicated to my mentors—thank you:

Dr. R. Dean Wright, Ph.D., Ellis and Nelle Levitt Professor Emeritus of Sociology, Department for the Study of Culture and Society, Drake University, helped me learn to reframe oppression and persecution to find a positive attitude. Dr. Dean provided undiluted feedback that helped me understand the constructs of discrimination, denial, scapegoating, theory and research methods. He helped me understand that I had a story to tell that would help other women who had been abused as children and ended up in prison and mental hospitals. He encouraged me to take writing courses and was patient as I struggled to put this story on paper.

Governor Robert D. Ray believed that I had changed my life. He returned my citizenship in 1974, granting me an executive pardon in 1982 and presented me with a reference letter in 1999. I promised him each time that I would not let him down and do the best I could to help the women in the Iowa criminal justice system.

Dr. Roxann Ryan, J.D., Ph.D., helped me find the confidence to attend graduate classes and turn my doubts into tenacity. She was an Assistant Iowa Attorney General when I met her and I was an ex-con. She helped me conceptualize my perception of *The Steel Ceiling* so I could present that paper at a sociological conference.

Joyce Brown, BA, MS, has always provided me with financial and emotional support. We even faced an abusive husband who had a gun together. I would not have been able to continue my education without her help. She has provided many years of comfort and a shoulder to cry on when things got bad, but she also told me to "get it together" when I wanted to feel sorry for myself.

Benjamin House, LISW, provided counseling through difficult phases. I continue to check in with him when I need to examine my motives or clarify blurred options.

Last, but certainly not least, this novel is dedicated to Terry L. Ruport. He supports my efforts to gain an education, write this novel and find my own answers.

PREFACE

When I was growing up on a farm, we raised chickens. When they were scared, they piled on top of each other and smothered the bottom chicks. As they grew older, they would pick the weak to death. That is how I visualize scapegoating.

CHAPTER 1

The United States was fighting World War II during the winter of 1945 when Beverly was born. Local newspapers supported patriotism by printing articles about youth going to or on leave from the war. Articles abounded about their deaths, injuries, and where they were prisoners. Everyone was urged to buy bonds and stamps.

Beverly's parents were still feeling the effects of the Great Depression. Her father had lost all of his savings when the banks closed; he worked for five cents a day when he could find work. Later, her second brother and first sister died. The additional miscarriage must have been horrible for her parents. She was real fortunate that they didn't give up trying to have children.

Her father idolized FDR for saving this country with the New Deal. Franklin's picture hung in their dining room until the house burned down in 1970. She was raised as a Democrat.

Male dominance in the middle of Iowa was unaffected by women working in factories for the war effort. Beverly's father was the only son in his family and didn't have to go to war. Her mother said he felt guilty about not doing his part. Her mother and most of the other women in their farming neighborhood were stay-at-home wives and mothers.

Women had only been able to vote for twenty five years in 1945, and abortions were still illegal. Women died or their babies were mentally defective or physically deformed from using coat hangers for illegal abortions.

Beverly was born in a hospital. According to local papers, the weather was fair with a high of forty-five degrees and a low of thirty one. Her mother told her that she was the first child in their family to be born in a hospital. The others were born at home and most had died.

There were four neighborhood children born within a few months that year. They lived within a mile of one another. They attended the same rural school together, but Beverly doesn't remember being particularly close to any of them.

Beverly's mother told her when she was growing up that she was born sucking on her fist, "The doctor told his nurse, 'Feed that kid!'" She said that Beverly never quit putting things in her mouth.

Beverly remembers her grandmother putting a "sugar-titty" on her thumb when she was very young and trying to shame her into not sucking it. She remembers acting like she was ashamed, but really wanted her grandmother to just finish tying the strips of fabric around her wrist so she could suck the dried sugar water out of the fabric.

Beverly's father, Ted, was born to John and Mary in 1913. He was the kindest hearted, most honest person Beverly has ever known. She could count on whatever he said to be the truth from his perspective. When he said yes, she knew she could count on him to do what he said. When he said no, she didn't ask again. He tried to teach her how to live with dignity, and he definitely taught her to die in faith and composure. How could a parent do more?

Ted, like his father, was a farmer and carpenter. Beverly remembers watching him start with a hole in the ground and a handshake to create beautiful homes for people. He laid block and brick, built custom cabinets, did the plumbing, electricity and plastered. He could do it all.

Her mother, Ann, told Beverly that Beverly knew the names of his tools before she could talk. He'd tell her, as a toddler, to go get him a wrench or something and she'd crawl up on his workbench to retrieve it.

John, her father's father, was a first generation American. His parents came to America on ships from Germany. They met and married here. Her great-grandparents died before Beverly was born, but Teddy, her older brother, told her that he didn't like their great-grandmother because he couldn't understand her.

Mary, Ted's mother, was a stay-at-home farm wife and mother. She gardened and cold-packed fruits, vegetables, and meat for the cave in their yard. She also made beautiful wedding band quilts that Beverly didn't appreciate until after her death. She taught Beverly to love flowers. Beverly spent lots of her youth helping Mary propagate African violets. Flower clubs came for lectures about those temperamental plants.

Mary also took great pride in her rock garden and fish pond until, as a toddler, Beverly jumped into the pond. The next time Beverly visited her grandparents, there were flowers blooming where the water had been.

Mary's parents were farmers. Their farm was on the outskirts of a Midwestern city. Mary's father died before Beverly was born, but her mother, Wilma, the "Little Witch", as Beverly called her, survived to make her holidays miserable for many years. Wilma was barely five feet tall and just as wide. She had a nasty disposition.

Beverly had gained quite a bit of weight after her sister, Becky, was born. There was a popular cigarette commercial at the time, "So round, so firm, so fully packed." Wilma seemed to find joy taunting Beverly with it and watching Ann grab Beverly's fist as she swung at her.

Ann said that Wilma had so many children that she tried to abort the two youngest, Fred and Bob, but missed. They had the mentalities of five- and seven-year-olds. When Beverly asked Ann how Wilma tried to abort them, Ann said that she had used a straightened clothes hanger, "That's the best way!"

As Beverly got older, she didn't like the mean way that John teased Fred and Bob. He made them feel bad, but Ann said that she was not to say anything. She never did.

Ann said that Ted's parents got married because Mary was

pregnant with Ted. She said that Mary's family never forgave John. She said that it hurt Ted that he wasn't named after John, per the custom at that time. Ted's younger brother, Jonathan, was named after his father, but he died as a youngster. Beverly remembers Mary was still crying about his death a few months before she died.

Ted had a sister, Jane, but her husband, Tim, kept her away from their family. She worked in an office and he was a night baker. Ann said they didn't have children because Tim gave Jane syphilis after his affair. He didn't tell her when they divorced. After they were remarried and she re-infected him, she got treated, but it was too late. She couldn't have children.

John, Ted, and Teddy built Jane a very nice two-bedroom brick home with an attached garage in the city. Unlike Beverly's home, which was cluttered and dusty most of the time, it was always very clean, not cluttered, and the furniture matched. Ann always told Beverly before they entered Jane's house, "You sit like a lady and don't you touch ANYTHING!"

Beverly must have been five or six the only time she remembers staying with Jane and Tim. She asked Tim if she could look at his large ruby and gold ring. She hid it under the corner of the sod by their house and wouldn't give it back to him for several days. Ann came to pick her up, "You go get that ring and give it to him!" Beverly dutifully complied, but doesn't remember being around them much after that.

Ann, Beverly's mother, was born to George and Sue in 1919. According to Ann, her parents were divorced when she was very young, "Divorce was an abominable stigma then." Sue, with the help of George's parents, raised Ann and her brother, Steve.

Ann told Beverly that she had two outfits growing up, one dress to wear to school and one for everyday. She also told Beverly that Mary, Ted's mother, taught her to cook after she and Ted were married because there was never enough food to waste when she was young. "Mama was afraid that I would ruin something and we wouldn't have anything to eat."

George moved to Pennsylvania after he and Sue were divorced. He remarried and owned a telephone company. He left everything to his second wife when he died. When she died, she left everything to the occult. Ann was devastated by the first rejection of the divorce, but more by the second. Leaving her out of his will wounded her deeply.

Sue, Ann's mother, was born in Nebraska. She was an LPN most of her life, did not remarry, and disliked men intensely. She had a negative attitude that made Beverly want to stay away from her.

Sue had arthritis and lived much of her later years in a wheelchair, creating beautiful crocheted doilies and tablecloths. She tried to teach Beverly to crochet numerous times, but Beverly was too busy being a tomboy. Sue taught her to chain, double and triple stitch with hook and thread, but Beverly told her that she had to go to the outside toilet and wouldn't come back inside until the next meal. Now, of course, Beverly wishes she had taken the time to learn.

Beverly doesn't know why Sue was raised by her cousins instead of her parents. Ann didn't talk very much about it. Apparently, during the period when Sue was a child, parents farmed their children out to other relatives when they couldn't afford to feed and clothe them. Sue must have felt rejected all of her life. First by her parents sending her to live with cousins when she was young, then being divorced, but the ultimate rejection must have been when Ted gave Ann the ultimatum that either Sue leave or he would.

Ann moved Sue in an apartment. She lived there alone, without a phone or wheelchair access, for years before her death. Of course, every Saturday Ann, Beverly and Becky went for groceries and to pick up whatever supplies Sue needed, but they seldom spent much time visiting with her.

Ann told Beverly that Sue died from leukemia. Beverly thinks it was from isolation and a broken heart.

Steve, Ann's brother, was an arrogant person that nobody in Beverly's family particularly liked, especially Ted. Ann said that Steve was married numerous times, but only had one daughter that no one ever met. Beverly thinks that's the reason she has no concept of what bonding with cousins would be like.

Steve seldom communicated with Beverly's family after Sue

moved from Los Angeles, where she had lived for many years, to Beverly's home. In fact, he called Ted and asked to talk to both Ann and Sue years after they died. Ted told Beverly that he said, "They're dead" and hung up.

Beverly spoke with Steve several times in the 1970s and got the impression that George was an alcoholic. She also concluded that Steve was too. Beverly visited with George's brother and his wife before they died. They confirmed that her grandfather was an alcoholic and that her uncle probably was. She thought that a possible reason for the many lapses in Steve communicating with her family was because he was in prison and didn't tell anyone.

Beverly remembers that Ann certainly had the co-dependent behaviors of a person who had been raised in that type of environment and Sue's face almost always had the expression of every new Alanon member: mad as hell!

Beverly remembers that Ann and Ted were not only husband and wife, they were partners in life. Ted almost giggled when he told Beverly about them getting married before Ann graduated from high school.

Beverly never heard either of them say a bad word to or about the other. There were no arguments. It got a little silent once in a while, but she learned to simply stay out of whatever was going on.

Ann enjoyed showing Beverly, time after time, the rented farm where Teddy was born. It was about a mile from John and Mary's farm. The story was always the same, "Then we bought the farm where we live now in 1939." It was eighty acres seven miles from the nearest town.

Beverly believes that Ted and Ann did the very best they could to make "family" a good experience because their childhoods had been so painful. However, they couldn't teach Beverly and her siblings the things they didn't know how to do. Neither of them got along with their siblings. How could they teach Beverly, Becky and Teddy to care about each other? They couldn't. They didn't know how.

Beverly has always loved being outside. She talked to the animals and explored the grove of trees that surrounded two sides of the farm buildings when she was very young. There was a wonderful pond next to the grove each time it rained. The soft slimy mud squished between her toes. Sometimes she'd belly-flop and get covered with mud. Ann washed her in the freezing water of the cistern before she'd let her back in the house.

The house was basically four square rooms that Ted had remodeled with a screened porch facing the gravel road and a windowed back porch that extended the full width of the house on the other side. Everyone entered the back porch door, walked through the porch and into the kitchen. To the left of the kitchen door was the door into Ted and Ann's bedroom. Ted built large drawers and a closet under the steps that led upstairs to Teddy's bedroom and the store room. Beverly slept in a bed behind their door; in front of the closet and drawers.

The kitchen and dining room were on the south side of the house. Ted took out the single door between them and made a wide arch. Likewise he replaced the door between the dining room and the living room with a large opening that included book shelves on the bottom facing the living room and square columns on the top. All three rooms seemed to flow into each other like one big L-shaped space.

Ted built a swivel television stand for their first small TV. It had doors on the bottom and sat in the dining room next to the kitchen. They turned it toward the kitchen at meal time and toward the living room for the evening. Too bad he didn't patent that idea.

The outside of the house was white with dark green wooden shingles above the front porch, the storm windows and screens were bright red, and the shingles on the rest of the house were blue. Ted liked bright colors.

The white square pump house was on the south side of the driveway that flanked the large shade trees in a row from the road to the garage. Its roof slanted. Its two small windows opened and served Beverly's fantasy purposes when she played store, bank, etc.

Once a robin used the window sill next to the driveway to build her nest so Beverly knew robins came out of eggs and looked ugly for the first few hours.

Ted drilled a very deep well, 365 feet, when they first moved to the farm. It provided some of the best drinking water in the area. There was always a bucket of drinking water with a dipper sitting on the kitchen counter by the porch door. If there were flies in it, Beverly dipped them out, throw them in the sink, and got a drink. The dirt from the gravel road always sank to the bottom of the pail and was no problem.

There was running water from the cistern for washing dishes and bathing in the galvanized tub that was stored on the back porch. It was a great day when the round tub that Beverly had to cross her legs to sit in was replaced by an oblong one that she could stretch out in.

Hogs and chickens were watered in the morning and evening from the cistern between the barn and corn crib. Beverly started out with one bucket about one-third full and worked her way up with age and strength to two five-gallon buckets completely full.

Actually, her first chore was to carry a small amount of fuel oil in a five gallon bucket to the house for the two heat stoves. The pump to the underground tank was behind the garage. The circular handle had to be turned many times before she got enough liquid to fill the stoves. Ann did the pouring because Beverly wasn't big enough to not spill it.

Ted built a beautiful red brick barn to the south of the house. Its curved roof extended almost to the ground. There were three rooms, the horse stall, the milking room, and the calf pen, on the east side of the center hall with the feed grinder by the north door. He ground grain for the cattle that spewed into bins in the feed room in the northwest corner. That's where Blackie, Beverly's dog that had rabies, was quarantined and died. Ted and a female neighbor had to have the shots because Blackie had licked open wounds on their hands.

The large room where cattle were fed in long bins by the hallway completed the west side. A wooden ladder was attached to the wall at the south end of the hall for access to the hay loft. It went almost to the roof where there was a bare bulb for light. There seemed to be all kinds of critters up there so Beverly stayed out.

Ted built a two story cement block garage with a wood burning stove for warmth, a big room for wood, a work bench, an overhead door for the car and a sliding door for the tractor. He used the second floor for storage. He mounted his drill press to the center column by the access opening. He also drilled holes for the drill bits in that column. Beverly used the bits as a ladder for access to the second floor. Ted couldn't understand why they kept getting bent. She confessed years later.

Beverly says she doesn't remember when the corn crib with a concrete floor, machine shed with a dirt floor, chicken and brooder houses with concrete floors were built. They were just always there.

Beverly didn't have an indoor bathroom growing up. They had an outhouse. It was northwest of the house when she was very young. She was afraid to use it because the wooden floor slanted toward the seat and gave way when she walked on it. It smelled really bad. She was afraid she was going to fall into the hole because it was far too big for her rear end.

Ted built a new toilet north of the garage. It had a concrete floor and two holes. He told her that the small one was for her. She remembers being able to go to the toilet after that.

They didn't use catalogs like some people did. They always had rolls of toilet tissue.

Beverly was not socialized to wash her hands after going to the toilet. It never was mentioned. Scooping manure from the barn, hog and chicken houses, or handling animals was probably more biologically dangerous. Ann told Beverly to wash her hands good before she ate, but even that was seldom enforced.

Taking turns bathing in four inches of water a couple times a week usually sufficed. If it was really hot, or Beverly was really dirty, she went to the cistern or washed up from the kitchen sink.

Ann used to tell Beverly that she was "head strong". Beverly thinks that she was probably right. Beverly's first memory consists of her sitting on her wooden potty chair by the wood cook stove in the kitchen. Ann, who was 5' 7" tall and a good 250 pounds, was shaking her finger in Beverly's face, "You're gonna sit there 'til you do your job!"

Thank goodness that Beverly, as a toddler, didn't have a large vocabulary or the abuse would probably have started that day. Her mental reaction was way beyond *GET OVER IT!*

Years later, Ann still got frustrated just talking about it, "The more I insisted that you go, the more you refused. I gave you laxatives and you didn't go. I gave you suppositories and nothing. And you just let out the water from the enemas!"

Do you suppose that it ever occurred to her that Beverly didn't need to go or that it might hurt after she stuck all of those things up her hind end?

Every time Beverly stayed with John and Mary, Mary braided her long, curly hair. Beverly would beg Mary each time to stop, "It hurts", but Mary would say, "That doesn't hurt. You hold still!" Then, when Beverly got home, Ann would take the braids out and pull the heck out of her hair. She'd scream and cry, but neither of them stopped.

As a toddler, Beverly probably wasn't developmentally capable of considering consequences. She had a small blue upholstered rocking chair and scissors in the living room one evening after the braids had been removed. Ann was doing dishes in the kitchen. Ted and Teddy weren't home. Beverly was mad and did what made sense to her. She got rid of the problem. She picked up the scissors, grabbed a hand full of hair with her left hand and cut it off by her ear. She put that hair on the floor in front of her and grabbed the other side of her hair and cut it off. She picked up the amputated cause of her pain and put it all behind the rocker. She sat down, smiled, and started rocking.

She yelled, "Mom, can I have a drink of water?"

Ann replied, "If you want a drink, come and get it!"

Beverly walked to Ann's right side. Ann looked down, dropped whatever she was washing into the water, and screamed, "What have you done?" She kept yelling and the next thing Beverly knew she was being thrown into her bed with Ann screaming something about killing her.

The bedroom door slammed as Ann left the room. The next thing Beverly remembers is being awakened with Ann pointing at her and screaming, "Do you see what she did?" Ted was looking down at her and Beverly wanted to crawl into the closet.

Beverly believes that she is lucky to have any hair at all today. Her hair grew back straight as a string. Ann took her to all kinds of beauticians. She had home perms, professional perms, and once she was even hooked up to some kind of electrical machine that burned her scalp. She continued to cut her hair short out of self-defense.

Funny, Beverly doesn't remember being spanked or even being yelled at that much as a toddler. She just knew to go to the barn for the Watkins salve that drew out the rocks, glass, or blood when she got cut or scraped. She didn't want Ann cleaning her wounds because it hurt.

Beverly enjoyed her first few years. She talked to the animals, wandered the fields, and kept her parents on their toes. Ann told her that when she was barely walking Ann saw her sauntering across the field one day, "The animals were following you in single file, the work horses, then the bull, the cattle, and then the hogs. You were talking and they were all just following you. I couldn't yell at you to come back because it might have stampeded them. I ran to the house and called Joy, the neighbor, to meet you at the fence. She picked you up while I drove up there."

Beverly didn't realize, even when Ann was telling her about it, how scared Ann had been. Three of Ann's children had died. Then she got this precocious, tenacious child that had a proclivity for ignoring danger.

Ted, who was less verbal than Ann, probably had the same fears. He had Beverly sitting on the top of one of the work horses that were hitched to the hay rack while he repaired the lane fence. Beverly remembers unsnapping the strap and yelling, "Gitty-up." The horses took off down the lane and she grabbed the two metal handles on the harness. She thought it was great fun until Ted stopped them. She doesn't remember being allowed to ride the horses after that.

A year or so later, Beverly was sitting in the cab of Ted's grain truck that was parked at the end of the lane. She opened the glove compartment and found his billfold. It had that green kind of money in it. She took it and walked into the corn field. The next thing she knew a big stranger grabbed her and started yelling, "I found her, Earl."

Beverly was kicking and screaming until Ted showed up. Ann told her years later that the big stranger was a neighbor who was slightly over five feet tall.

Beverly was a pretty outgoing child. She doesn't remember being scared very often. Once, during one of Ted's softball games when the lights went out and she couldn't find him, she yelled, "Daddyyyy?" There were a lot of men laughing, but Ted scooped her up and hugged her. She was safe again.

Beverly doesn't remember Ann hugging her and making her feel safe, only Ted did that. And he quit after her sister was born. Years later, Beverly asked Ann's best friend about it and she told Beverly that she and her mother were watching Beverly when she was small. Beverly was throwing one of her numerous on-the-floor, kicking and screaming tantrums. The older woman picked Beverly up and rocked her. She said that Beverly stopped her tantrum.

Ann's best friend said that she didn't remember Ann hugging Beverly either, "Maybe she didn't know how because she never got that when she was young."

Beverly got really good at finding the puppies and kittens after they were born. Ann said that the mothers would kill them if she held the babies too early, but they never did. But then, Beverly waited for the mothers to clean them. Usually, the mother was having another one so she didn't mind. The animals let Beverly hug them. Somehow she felt safer with them than she did with people.

Ann said that Beverly wouldn't speak to Ted for weeks after he took Buster, an all white dog with long hair, to the grove and shot him because he was old. Beverly remembers being mad at him about it and turning her head away when he tried to talk to her. Then he gave her a piglet. Teddy told Beverly, years later, that she was a runt that Ted didn't expect to live. She did live! Teddy also said that she was the biggest sow they ever raised.

All Beverly knows is that Babs followed her around like a puppy after she fed her with a baby bottle. They had wonderful times and conversations, "Okay, so she grunted and I did my toddler babble, but we understood each other. It's called love."

Babs was having her first litter. Beverly was sitting on the straw petting her face while she was delivering the second one. Ted came into the hog house and gently told Beverly to come to him. She tried to explain that Babs needed her to love her, but he insisted. Beverly told Babs, "I'll be right back" and walked to Ted. He grabbed her up and took her outside. "Don't you EVER get into a pen with a sow having pigs! They will eat you!!"

"But it's Babs! She needs me!"

Ted was sterner than she had ever known, "Don't you EVER do THAT again!"

She didn't.

The chicken house had a fenced-in pen to the south. One day Beverly watched as a rooster was jumping on top of the hens and pecking their heads. She knew that the baby chicks weren't supposed to do that because it killed them. She figured that the big chickens weren't supposed to behave that way either. She got a bucket, unhooked the gate, walked into the chicken pen and chased the rooster. There was a terrible commotion as the chickens flew and squawked. Ann came out of the house and yelled at her to stop. Beverly pointed at the culprit, but Ann didn't seem to understand his crime. She grabbed the bucket out of Beverly's hand, took her out of the pen, said that the rooster was making babies, and walked away.

Beverly related her thoughts, "How could that be? Baby chicks come out of eggs. I watched them. Babies came out of animals. I watched them. The cows and pigs didn't peck heads. Sure wish I'd have known how to ask her all of that stuff, but she just went back into the house leaving me to ponder what the heck she was talking about."

Beverly went to school in a rural town. The downtown consisted basically of two blocks in an L-shape. There were as many bars as there were churches, maybe more at times. There were two brick yards, a saw mill, and a bean plant. The kids at school were divided mainly into farm kids or their parents worked at one of those businesses. There was one girl in Beverly's class that was rich and wore really nice clothes, but the rest pretty much wore what they had.

Kindergarten was all right. Beverly enjoyed lying on the rug during nap time. She really liked the bottles of chocolate milk and peanut butter sandwiches. Ann said that they mixed the peanut butter with honey in those sandwiches. Beverly asked if they could do that at home, but Ann said she didn't like peanut butter that way so they couldn't.

Teddy told Ann to make Beverly quit crawling under the school bus seats and kissing her neighbor. Beverly just looked at Ann and thought, "Well, what am I supposed to do on that long trip?" Of course, she didn't say anything, just glared at Teddy.

Climbing on an icy jungle gym is not a good idea. Beverly ended up bleeding from her crotch after she fell. She was scared, in excruciating pain, and crying. The next thing she remembers is Ann taking her to the doctor. He told Beverly that she was going to be all right, but Ann looked worried. Years later, Ann told Beverly that she had lost her virginity that day and was not supposed to be able to have children.

May Basket time was frustrating because Teddy's friends would never let Beverly catch them so she could kiss them. That's what Ann said she was supposed to do.

Teddy didn't like Beverly. He and his friend made a hole in a snow drift, put her in it and walked away. Ann finally rescued her.

Beverly doesn't remember Teddy ever sitting and talking with her. In fact, years later he told her that he'd let her follow him into the grove, circle around and back to the house, leaving her lost in the grove.

Beverly learned that there wasn't a Santa Claus before her sister was born. The Christmas Eve neighborhood party was at their house that year. She was busy fixing a plate of cookies that she and Ann had baked that day for Santa. The older kids started laughing at her and telling her that Ted and Ann put the gifts out after she went to sleep. They called her stupid and other names that made her cry.

Ann scolded them, but the damage had been done. It took Beverly a few more years to transfer that concept to the Tooth Fairy and Easter Bunny.

Her little sister was smarter than she was. She didn't admit to not believing in Santa until after she was married. She received gifts from both Santa and Ted every year.

Beverly got into a lot of trouble as a toddler. Ted told her to stay out of the field while they were bailing hay. Yeah, like that was going to happen. Well, she stepped in some kind of hornet's nest and rapidly became a mass of stings. Joy rescued her again and put baking soda paste on each puncture. Teddy teased her so much that she was trying to lock herself in the car to get away from him, but the door slammed on her thumb and she couldn't get it open or pull it out. He stood there laughing until Ann came and opened the door. She later lost the nail. Not a good day for the kid!

Ann told Beverly that Ted was going to make a bedroom for her across the hall from Teddy's room; replacing the storeroom. Beverly was excited and a little bit scared of sleeping by herself in a big room, but Ann assured her that Teddy would be across the hall. Beverly remembers, "Yeah, like that made me feel secure?"

Ted had custom built a one-door closet, a desk with drawers and nooks, and cabinets with plywood doors and several dresser drawers under the rafters on the north wall of Teddy's room. In the same manner he constructed a dresser in the middle of a two-door closet and toy chest. The toy chest also had two drawers under the doors. Ann put up frilly curtains and a toy patterned linoleum on the floor. Beverly's night light was round with a tent, camp fire and woods. The inside turned around so the smoke looked like it was rising out of the camp fire. Beverly watched it until she fell asleep.

About the same time Ann sat Teddy and Beverly down. "You're going to have a brother or sister," she said gleefully.

Teddy looked at her, said, "How could you!?" and walked away.

All Beverly knew is that he was mad so she was supposed to be, too. Later she was taken to their neighbor's home to wait for Ann to have the baby. Beverly was happy because she was getting a baby…pig, puppy, kitten, calf, chicken? Nope! It was red and crying when Ann laid it on her lap. "This is your sister. You love her."

Beverly looked at it, "I hate it!"

"You can't!" Ann yelled as she caught Becky sliding off of her lap, "You have to love her! She's your sister!!"

Beverly knew that Teddy hated it and so did she. She went outside.

A few days later, Ann was in bed during the day. Beverly started to crawl in with her, but Ann shoved her away. It was a shock, as she hit the floor, because Ann had never pushed her away with such force before.

Years later, Ann told her that she had mastitis and any movement or pressure was excruciating. All Beverly knew at the time was that since that baby showed up, she was alone and "it" was getting all of the attention.

Beverly gained a lot of weight after Becky was born. Her school pictures are testimony of this. She started to withdraw and stay by herself more. Ann made her clothes or bought "tubby" clothes for her. Beverly was teased a lot about being fat by the other kids.

Beverly was not very nice to Becky at first. She mostly ignored her, but at some point she started feeling protective of her. When Becky started walking she followed Beverly wading in the mud by the grove after a rain, they baked cookies in the sun on Teddy's wooden rabbit hutch. Vanilla was made with the saw dust from Ted's electric saw and water, chocolate from dirt and water. Beverly drew the line when her neighbor made butterscotch with cow manure.

There was a tree in the grove that had two trunks growing perpendicular to the ground. Beverly cut off the horse heads from their riding sticks and Ted nailed them to the tree trunks. Becky and Beverly jumped up and down on the limbs like they were riding horses and pretended adventures.

Beverly's family spent every Sunday with John and Mary. Either they drove the twenty some miles to their farm, or John and Mary came to their home. John started holding Beverly more after Becky was born. Beverly thought it felt good because everyone else was holding Becky. He started taking her for walks and touching her in ways that she sometimes liked and sometimes it hurt. Her butt got sore because her mouth wouldn't open far enough for him. Later, he promised her that she could have a pony if she sucked him, "Mama and daddy haven't said it's all right yet. As soon as they agree, I will buy you a pony." He even gave her a bridle before her birthday one time. She held the bridle, sat on Teddy's green 4-H trunk and cried, but she never got the pony. He kept making promises and she continued to believe him and be disappointed.

She refused to go into the corn crib with him after he really hurt and nobody asked her why.

First grade was interesting. She was put in something that Ann called an accelerated class. She told Beverly that she would be in a class with second graders who were smart. Ann said that she was a peacock.

Beverly recalls, "Now I'm sure that all made sense to her, but I didn't even know what a peacock was, let alone the concept behind it. I just dutifully went to school."

It was a cold day, one of those days that the rain and sleet caused your bones to chill clear through. Beverly talked a second grader into running away with her. They walked from the school house to the river in the sleet before he wanted to go back. She walked back to within a block of the school with him, but she saw her parents standing in the street. He walked on and she lay down in the cold ditch water. She didn't know where she wanted to go, but she didn't want to go back. Her memory ends there.

Beverly was eight when a gas company arrived. Their farm sat on top of several porous underground rock formations. Ann said that the domed rocks were filled with water and would be a natural storage for natural gas.

Their farm, and the farms around them, started looking like an oil field. Tall drills lit up the sky at night. Beverly was about nine when the gas mains were being laid and the gas was turned on and flowing.

Of course, by that time the drill mud had contaminated their well and they had to boil the water so it was safe for human consumption. The animals just had to endure.

About the same time Teddy married Diane, a shy petite blond, and moved to the city. Beverly moved into his room and Becky took over the room they had shared.

Diane's brother and sister taught Beverly to smoke cigarettes in the bedroom while the wedding ceremony was happening. They also told her how to steal packs of cigarettes in grocery stores and not get caught.

One day Becky, who was about three, caught John masturbating Beverly in their kitchen. The rest of the family was in the living room. Becky looked at his hand and then his face. Beverly looked at his face too. He was smiling and his hand didn't stop. Becky looked back at his hand, her face, and then his face again. He was still smiling and she smiled back at him. Beverly thought, *Oh, no you don't!*

After Beverly's grandparents left she told Ann what John had been doing to her and that he was going to start hurting Becky, too. Ann told her, "You stay away from Grandpa and don't tell Daddy. It will hurt him."

Beverly's life changed that day. Today Beverly understands the concept of denial, but at nine she didn't understand. In retrospect, this is what she believes happened. Ann craved a family life because she was the product of divorced parents. In Ann's mind, Beverly's announcement corrupted the happy family fantasy she and Ted were providing for their children.

The mental and physical abuse slowly escalated from that day on. No matter what Beverly did, it was never enough for Ann. Ann's favorite sentence to her was, "You are not living up to your potential!" She never explained what her potential was so Beverly had no idea how to do it.

Beverly had always blamed herself for not telling Ann what John was doing sooner, but today she understands that she was developmentally incapable of abstract thought until that moment. Besides, she wanted that pony. Only when she realized that he was going to hurt Becky did she tell. It wasn't her fault. John was the predator.

Beverly remembers starting off each new school year trying to do the best she could, but kids called her things like "smarty fatty" and she would quit trying and eat more. Once she brought home a report card with four As and one B. Ann looked at it and pointed at the B, "Why isn't this one an A?"

Beverly was confused. She remembered that she had really tried, but after Ann's question, she knew that she would never be good enough. She quit trying again.

Beverly's family, along with John and Mary, started spending some Sundays at Teddy and Diane's apartment. Sandy was born and everyone fussed over her and Becky.

Beverly would take Sandy out of John's arms and hand her to someone else, but no one asked her why. She would drag Becky off of John's lap, but no one asked her why. She didn't want him to hurt Sandy or Becky like he hurt her. She also made sure that he wasn't alone with Becky. It was a big job for a young girl to keep John from hurting anybody every Sunday.

Somewhere in here Beverly showed her neighbor how John had masturbated her, but neither of them liked it so they quit.

Beverly learned to ride a bike so she could get away from Becky because she could not ride her tricycle on the road. Man, did Beverly ever have trouble getting the hang of balancing that thing! She used most of the Watkins salve in the barn pulling the rocks out of her legs and arms after she skidded across the driveway and road. Finally her neighbor, who was two years younger, much thinner, and had been riding a bike for several years, suggested that Beverly stand rather than sit. That worked. Later she learned to sit on the seat without falling over.

Beverly did not particularly like human babies. Becky liked dolls. Beverly was more interested in the animals, guns, holsters, etc. She would put her dolls that she received for Christmas up in the cabinet and bribe Becky into doing her chores before she gave them to her.

Teddy moved back to the farm and Beverly moved back into Becky's room with her. He and Diane got a divorce and he started bringing Kim, a boisterous and aggravating brunette, home for the weekends. Ann told Beverly that she did not like Kim because she made Teddy leave his wife and daughter. She also told Beverly that Kim, who worked with Teddy, would wait in his car for a ride home. Once Diane found Kim in the car and Teddy still gave Kim a ride home. Ann told Beverly that she was disappointed in Teddy for allowing Kim to come between him and his family.

Kim slept with Beverly on weekends until she tried to put Beverly's hand between her legs one night and Beverly yelled, "NO!" in the middle of the night.

Ann wanted to know what was going on and Kim said, "Nothing." Ann said that she caught Kim coming out of Teddy's room later so she was not allowed to stay with them anymore.

Beverly was relieved because she got an icky feeling every time Kim was around.

Teddy told Beverly that she could be in his wedding to Kim if she would tell the priest that he had never been married. Teddy and Kim took Beverly to a big church in the city where they all talked to a man with a funny collar. He asked Beverly a lot of questions. Teddy and Kim motioned for Beverly to answer yes or no and then the man asked her the question that sealed her fate of being in their wedding, "Has he ever been married?"

Beverly dutifully said, "No," and the questioning was over.

Today she wonders why a priest would accept the word of an adolescent in such a matter. Didn't he think that it was funny that Teddy's parents weren't there giving this testimony?

If Beverly would have known what being in their wedding meant, she would have told that man the truth. She didn't especially enjoy getting dressed in the tight satin dress, hose, and heels that she couldn't walk in. Nor did she enjoy Kim's attitude toward her.

Beverly's whole family talked for years about how drunk Kim, her brother, and the priest got after the ceremony.

Ann never liked Kim. She caught Kim in Ann's bedroom, taking the tablecloths and doilies that Sue had crocheted out of the dresser. Ann threw Kim out of the bedroom and told her to never go back into that room again. That only worked while Ann was alive. After her death, Kim emptied the drawers under the stairway of the fabric Ann had saved for sewing clothes for Beverly and Becky.

Kim and Beverly pretty much got along like fire and gasoline. Ann told Beverly to tolerate her to keep family peace. She did most of the time, but she never trusted her.

Beverly was about twelve. She and a town girl left the football game and walked downtown. A car with two boys stopped. The town girl told her to get into the front seat while she and one of the boys got into the back. They rode around while noises came from the back seat.

Beverly listened to the driver and ignored the noises. He drove out of town and stopped on a gravel road. He slid over and started kissing Beverly while his hands squeezed her breast and clit. She started crying and couldn't stop. He got mad and the town girl directed him to drive her home. He slammed the car to a stop in her driveway, opened the door, and shoved her out. The car threw dust and rocks as it sped away.

Ann opened the porch door and started screaming at Beverly to get into the house. Beverly ran to the door with tears streaming down her cheeks. She wanted to tell Ann what had happened and be held. Instead, Ann grabbed Beverly's arm, dragged her to the bedroom and threw her on the bed. The next thing Beverly knew Ann was beating her with Ted's leather belt and screaming, "Cry, damn you, cry!"

Something died in Beverly that night. She felt it go dead. From that night on, if she did not want to deal with something, she simply chose not to feel anything.

Beverly isn't sure how long Ann hit her or what else she yelled. The only thing she remembers is Ted pulling Ann away. "You're going to kill her, Ann!" He held her while she cried and Beverly went to her room in silence.

Beverly doesn't remember talking about that night with Ann. The particulars simply compounded the aggregate of pain Beverly stuffed. She continued to make sure that John didn't hurt her or Becky, but Ann accelerated her abuse. They seemed to settle into a pattern. Ann would send Becky outside so she could talk to Beverly. That was the signal that Beverly was about to be either mentally, emotionally, or physically beat to a pulp, usually all three.

Beverly found that she could get the pain over with by making some remark that escalated Ann faster. One day, Ann was on some kind of a kick about all the things that were wrong with Beverly. Beverly yelled, "Are you sure you got the right baby in the hospital?" Yup, beating done, Ann would cry and say that she would never do that again, and Beverly could get on with her chores.

Beverly met a 28-year-old man from a neighboring town. He had beer and wanted sucked. She found that beer made the pain go away for a while so she wanted beer and he didn't want anything different than John wanted. Well, at least he didn't want to stick that thing in her butt and hurt her that way, too.

She started using the school bus as a cab into town. She just called her friend instead of going to school. He came and picked her up or she hid at somebody's house until he got off of work. The Sheriff got pretty good at hunting her down each time Ann called him so she started going to the city and staying lost longer.

Ann told Beverly that the sheriffs from two counties had told her to lock Beverly away and forget that she ever had her. That sounded good to Beverly, but she was never allowed to say anything to Ann without suffering the consequences so she stayed silent.

Beverly was thirteen when the gas company constructed the large compressor station and dehydration plant a little over a mile north of her house. She doesn't remember what year it was that the gas got away from them. All she remembers is that there were three spewing geysers about a quarter of a mile southeast of her house. The gas and water blew for days from the "Old Faithful"-looking spouts.

Beverly was raised in the Methodist church. Between the times she ran away, she did her chores, taught Sunday school to 3-year-olds, and sang in the choir. She isn't sure what the minister said, but what she heard was that Jesus loved her and God was going to punish her. She knew that what John had been doing was wrong, what she was doing with other guys was wrong, and she was going to burn in hell for eternity.

Ann saved Beverly's life once. Ted had back surgery to fuse two discs and could no longer do the field work and chores. Ann and Beverly took over those responsibilities. Ted decided to get rid of the animals to make it easier for Ann and Beverly. All of the animals were gone except the sows.

Beverly was in the hog pen with her neighbors to load the last of the sows into the stock truck. The last to be loaded was the biggest. This one always had a real bad attitude. Beverly had been feeding them for months and this sow attacked her almost every day, only this time she didn't have a bucket in her hands to protect herself.

Beverly was standing between the corn crib and the hog waterer. She heard Ann scream, "Look out, Beverly!"

She instinctively knew what was happening and simply reacted. She jumped over the five-foot high wooden fence headfirst. She heard the sow hit the fence while she was above it. She landed on the back of my neck and shoulders and flopped to a halt. There was no doubt in her mind that the sow would have made mince meat out of her if Ann hadn't yelled at her. Years later, she found out that she broke her collarbone that day.

Beverly stayed with Ann's first cousin, Jerry, and his wife a few days every summer. He owned an implement company. She walked the few blocks from their house to his business to watch the mechanics work on machinery. She'd tell them, "Daddy wouldn't do that." They'd tell Beverly to go tell Jerry that he wanted her.

She asked one of them for a drink of water one day. He told her that there was a water fountain in the men's restroom. She was walking toward it when Jerry asked her where she was going. She told him. He handed her some change and glared at the mechanic, "Go get a bottle of pop and I'll take care of these smart-alecks."

She asked, "Why's everybody laughing?"

Jerry shook his head. "Beverly, it's a urinal not a water fountain!" Then, of course, he had to explain what a urinal was.

There was a Shetland pony farm on the south edge of town. Beverly was too fat to catch one so the town kids would catch one and bridle it for her to ride bare back. She begged Ann and Ted to buy one for her, but they never did. Neither did John.

Jerry took Beverly to their cabin on Twin Lakes after work most evenings. He pushed the wooden raft seated on tractor tubes out in the water and they dived off of it. The water was cool after the suffocating humid summer days. His wife didn't go with them. She seemed to tolerate her visits, but seldom spoke to her.

Jerry was funny and made her feel welcome. He never tried anything funny with her. She was grateful to him for that. She could feel safe with at least one other man than Ted.

Beverly doesn't remember hearing an argument between any of

her family. It wasn't allowed. Ann would go off at her regularly when they were by themselves, but silence was more the habit in their family.

Years later, Beverly asked Ted what he and Ann argued about. He looked at her like he couldn't believe she asked the question, "Why would we argue?"

"Didn't you ever disagree?"

"Yeah."

"What did you do?"

"We talked about it," he said as if she was already supposed to know the answer.

It was her turn to look astonished, "How did I miss that concept?"

Beverly started stealing cigarettes again after Teddy married Kim and moved out of the house the second time. She had been stealing his. Now grocery stores were the norm. Their next door neighbors also donated a pack here and there. Their daughter and Beverly smoked in their hay loft by the open door that was on the side away from their house. Beverly told her father many years later while they were drinking in a bar. He couldn't believe that they hadn't started the barn on fire, "It would have enveloped you!"

Ann drove Beverly and Becky to Perry every Saturday. They stopped to see Sue to get her list for groceries and the other items she needed. They would small talk, Sue would show them what she was crocheting, and they'd leave. Beverly swung with her usual Saturday pack of L&Ms from the grocery store and went to the car to wait for Ann to finish her shopping.

Ann and Becky came out of the store. Becky got in the back seat and Ann put the groceries in the trunk. Ann slammed a carton of L&Ms on the front seat as she entered the car. She didn't say a word, but her jaw was set and Beverly knew she was mad. Neither of them mentioned the cigarettes until after they had delivered Sue's items and were on the road home.

Beverly's mind raced as they rode in silence. There had to be a logical explanation. Let's see, Teddy smoked L&Ms. She asked, "Did Teddy ask you to buy him some cigarettes?"

Ann's jaw tightened. "Nope!"

Ted had smoked cigarettes in the hospital instead of his pipe. Maybe he liked them better and was switching to cigarettes. "Are they for Daddy?"

"Nope!"

Beverly was out of options so she just quit asking.

Ann waited the appropriate amount of time to let her sweat, then, "I had to pay for the cigarettes you took. I will buy you a carton of cigarettes a week, but if you EVER steal anything else I will kill you!"

Beverly acted like she was really sorry, but a whole carton a week? She had been lucky to steal a couple packs a week. Ann had just handed her a bonanza. She never stole another pack of cigarettes and she even quit stealing candy from the dime store. Well, most of the time.

Beverly ran away a lot. Sometimes it was just easier than dealing with John or Ann trying to get her alone and hurt her. It got so bad that she even forgot that she wasn't there to protect Becky. She just couldn't do it any longer, but she had told John that she would kill him if he hurt Becky the way he did her.

Beverly was fourteen the first time Ann took her to a psychiatrist. She told Beverly on the way that she would kill her if she told him anything about what John was doing to her or their "disagreements." Beverly had no reason to not believe her because it felt like she had come pretty close a couple of times.

Beverly sat in the waiting room. She thought, *So this is what it feels like to be nuts. Wonder how it feels to be all right. Wonder what they are going to do to me now. Will it hurt? Will they finally get me killed? What do I have to do to be good enough?*

Beverly was escorted into an office. The man asked her a few questions and she answered them as best she could. It shocked her when he asked, "Do you hate your mother?"

"NO!" she answered dutifully. Actually, she had never thought about what hate was.

"Are you sure?" he continued.

She didn't answer. She thought to herself that she would be wrong to hate Ann. She probably hated John, but no, she was just scared of him. Then, too, she was scared of Ann. What did hate mean? If it meant scared of the person, then maybe she did hate them, but she didn't answer because she didn't know how to answer. It seemed to her that nobody liked her. The people she was supposed to be able to trust hurt her or ignored her like Ted did. She just emotionally left the conversation. She didn't know how long the man talked. The next thing she was aware of, he was saying that she could go home.

On the way home, Ann told Beverly that the doctor had given her three prescriptions. She said that she would make aluminum foil packets for Beverly to take to school. Beverly didn't answer.

Every morning Ann handed Beverly the aluminum foil packet with the pills. The first day she forgot. The second day she gulped the two packets down at the water fountain and got on the bus for home. By the time she got there she didn't care what Ann said to her. She did her choirs, took the pills at supper, and relaxed. Actually, the pills got rid of the pain almost as well as beer did. She didn't have to suck anybody for them either.

Beverly continued to run away, usually after an especially difficult Sunday trying to keep John away from her and Becky.

Once when Beverly came home to Ann's usual tirade and screaming, she screamed back, "Why is it all right for grandpa to do whatever he wants to me, but its not all right when I want to do it with other men?" After she got slapped around for awhile and watched while Ann cried, she was sent to her room.

Beverly was fifteen or sixteen when Ann and Ted took her to court for being incorrigible. They sat in the judge's chambers. Ann explained how Beverly ran away all of the time for no reason, that they had spent money they didn't have so she could have counseling and medication, and nothing seemed to work.

The judge scolded Beverly for not appreciating her wonderful parents. He was in the process of telling her that he was going to send her to the state girls facility when Ann interrupted, "Oh no! Her father and I will take responsibility for her!"

Beverly's head exploded, *Who's nuts around here? Get me*

away from this bitch!! but she couldn't speak. She didn't want to pay the price when Ann got her alone again.

Beverly started praying that Ann would die that day. She knew that was the only way that she would ever get away from her. Somebody always took her back to Ann to be hurt again and again when she ran away.

The judge put Beverly on probation and gave custody to Ann and Ted. Beverly didn't understand, "Didn't they already have custody of me? What's the difference? Is somebody going to make people quit hurting me?"

Ted was on the school board. Beverly was not doing well in public school so she was sent to a business college in the city to learn business machines. She really didn't fit in with people who had graduated from high school. She walked away and got drunk.

Some place in this time frame Beverly had a date. A real date where he picked her up at the farm, met her parents, the whole bit. He was not very attractive and he had dried soap in his ears. Yuk! She ditched him in the city and picked up a man in a bar, went home with him, and the sheriff woke them the next morning.

Ann told Beverly that the man was going to jail for statutory rape and Beverly told Ann that if she did anything to him that she would never speak to her again. "What is the difference between him and Grandpa?"

Ann had loaned Beverly her watch for the date. Sue had given it to her for graduation from high school. Well, she couldn't afford it when Ann actually graduated so she had given it to her several years before. Beverly needed money after she ditched her date so she hocked it.

Ann asked for her watch after Beverly returned home. She told Ann what she had done. Ann told her to get cleaned up and she drove her to the store. She stopped the car, reached in front of Beverly and opened the door. "Come home with my watch." Beverly climbed out, closed the door, and Ann drove off.

Beverly stood there in disbelief for a while. She thought Ann was trying to scare her. She thought that Ann would drive around the block, but that didn't happen.

That was the day that Beverly learned how much money men would pay for sex. She went home with Ann's watch. She didn't ask Beverly how she paid for it and Beverly didn't tell her.

About the same time Ann hit Beverly one more time. Beverly doesn't remember why, but this time she didn't fly across the room or fall to the floor like she usually did. She simply took the punch, her eyes went dead. "That's the last time, Mom!" She was taken to a private mental hospital.

It was Beverly's sixteenth birthday. The psychiatrist was going to give her a shock treatment. She told him that it was her birthday. He didn't care. He said happy birthday and everything went black. She came back to awareness that afternoon with a horrible headache. Ann had left a birthday cake and a ceramic doll dressed like a southern bell. This is the only memory Beverly has of that period, until the day she left. Ann told her that she had sixteen shock treatments.

Beverly was sent back to school. She couldn't concentrate or study. She doesn't remember anything except disorientation. The kids wouldn't talk to her on the bus or at school. Years later, Becky told her that she was embarrassed because the other kids made circular motions around their ears that meant "nuts" and pointed at Beverly. Teddy refused to talk to her.

One day Ann admonished Beverly for not saying hello to her neighbor. She asked who the neighbor was and Ann hit her. "Don't you get smart with me!" Beverly didn't know who she was talking about because nothing made any sense after the shock treatments, but she wouldn't admit that she didn't know something again.

Beverly was already introverted, but she put up more emotional armor against the constant beatings she was taking. She never felt safe and there was nowhere she could run to escape. Someone always found her and returned her to people who hurt her. Ann would kill her if she told anyone and was probably going to kill her if she didn't.

Ted made Beverly learn to drive the car in the oat field around the oat shocks before she could drive on the gravel roads. It wasn't difficult because she had been driving the tractor for years. Then he made her change a tire and the oil. She had watched him do these things for years and was happy to finally be able to perform these tasks herself.

Beverly was just as irresponsible with the car as she had been with everything else she touched. She drove fast, drank as much beer as she could hold, took the prescribed medications, and came home when she pleased. Since Ted's tools were in the trunk and he didn't trust her having access to them, he didn't give the key to the trunk.

First she ripped the muffler and tailpipe off because she went over the railroad tracks too fast and bounced. She picked them up and put them in the back seat. Next she ruined a tire by driving on it while it was flat and split it all the way around the sidewall.

Beverly had lost a lot of weight when she got the shock treatments. More guys seemed to want to have sex with her rather than her just sucking them. She found out what it meant to be sexually satisfied. She liked it.

Beverly knew she was pregnant the night she had sex with her neighbor. She also knew that Ann was probably going to kill her when she found out. Beverly told the neighbor that she was pregnant and he told her that he was married and not the father. She got drunk and ran Ted's car into a tree. She had meant to kill herself, but only wrecked the car and had a sore head and knee.

Ann and Ted took Beverly to the doctor. She told him that she was pregnant. She told him in confidence, but he told Ann. Beverly was taken back to the "nut ward" in the city.

By this time Beverly was totally passive-aggressive. She refused to speak until Ann showed up a few days later to tell her that she was pregnant. Beverly shook her head, knowing that Ann could not beat her. "You couldn't believe me? You had to kill a rabbit?"

Ann told Beverly that she was going to have an abortion. Beverly said, "If you force me to have an illegal abortion I'll go to every newspaper in this country until somebody prints my story. You are not going to kill my baby!" She had no idea how prophetic that was.

Instead of an abortion, Ann decided that Beverly would go to an unwed mother's home in the city. She said, "You will stay here until your baby is born. Then it will be put up for adoption."

Beverly didn't say anything. She stayed for a couple days. She listened to other girls who were close to delivering their babies talk about how much they didn't want to give them up for adoption. She realized that she would rather they both die than go through the emotional pain those girls were describing. She walked away from the facility.

Beverly doesn't remember where she met the man she stayed with, probably at some bar. All she remembers is that he had four children. One was older than she was. He was kind and she appreciated not being yelled at, beaten, and hurt.

A few days later Beverly called the unwed mother's home to see if she could get her clothes. Ann and Ted were there packing her things. Ann got on the phone and told her that she could come home, have her baby, and keep it. Beverly was overjoyed. The man dropped her off a couple of blocks from the facility and she walked the rest of the way.

The next few months were better. Ann was more relaxed. It seemed to Beverly that since the worst thing that could ever happen had already happened, Ann had accepted her and her baby.

Ann made Beverly wear the wedding band she bought her. Beverly shook her head as she put it on and thought to herself, *Like everybody doesn't know that I'm not married?*

Ann talked to Beverly about the birthing process and explained that it would hurt, "But the more you do what the doctors and nurses tell you to do, the faster it will happen and it will hurt for a shorter time."

Those were the best months Beverly remembers for a lot of years. Ann and she talked about everything. Ann told her about the problems she had with her when she was a toddler and Beverly told her what she remembered about those years. Ann said she didn't realize that small children had those types of memories. Ann refused to discuss Beverly's molestation, but told her that Mary had talked about how much sex with John hurt her. Beverly thought to herself, *I know how much he can hurt someone*. Ann was still talking, "I told her to get some lubricant."

While Beverly was pregnant, it was hard for her to get to and from the outside toilet. One night she fell on the ice. She lay there like a turtle on her back. She couldn't flip over to get any traction. She yelled and screamed for help, but no one could hear her with the windows closed and the television on. Finally, Ann came to the door and yelled to see if she was all right. Ann and Ted came to her rescue and helped her get back in the house.

Beverly had to get cleaned up. She had urinated herself lying on the ice. She was almost frozen to the ground. How embarrassing!

Ted started the addition on the house the next day. He built a beautiful bedroom for them and a bathroom and hallway where their bedroom had been.

On Beverly's 17th birthday, she was taken to the hospital in the city to have labor induced. She lay there with a needle in her arm and talked to her baby, but nothing happened. She was sent home. The next few days she had some discomfort, but still no real pain.

Beverly was sleeping on the couch in the living room four days later. Ann and Ted had their bed in the dining room while he completed the new bathroom and bedroom. Beverly awoke about 1:00 a.m. with a numb pain in her back. She woke Ann. "This feels different."

Ann started timing the pains and called the doctor about 4:00 a.m. He told her to bring Beverly to his office. The next thing Beverly knew she was in the back seat of the car with Becky while Ted drove slowly over the buckled concrete so he didn't hurt her. They arrived at the doctor's office. He examined Beverly and she was rushed into his station wagon with Ann in the front seat. He drove so fast that it seemed he only hit the tops of the buckled concrete.

They arrived at the hospital and Beverly was rushed into a room where her pubic hair was shaved off. She was afraid she was going to drop the baby in the toilet after the enema, but the nurse assured her that she would not.

The next thing Beverly remembers is lying in bed listening to the woman in the next room screaming. She asked Ann and the doctor, "Is it going to get that bad?"

Ann shook her head that it wouldn't and the doctor said, in disgust, "It's her fourth one and she does this every time."

The doctor broke Beverly's water and the pains intensified, but panting like a dog made them bearable. Then she relaxed and went to sleep until the next one. Those intervals shortened and she started emotionally leaving like she did when John and Ann hurt her. Once, during a particularly hard pain, Beverly saw her baby using her hands and arms to part the canal and crawl toward the opening. Beverly started laughing while she panted. Ann looked worried and asked if she was all right. After the pain stopped, Beverly told Ann what she visualized and they both laughed.

A man came into the room and gave Beverly a shot that he called a "spinal." After that, there was no pain. In fact, there was no feeling at all below her waist. She was taken to the delivery room, put into stirrups, and her beautiful daughter was born. Beverly was sewn up and taken to her room.

Beverly didn't get to hold her baby. Nor did she get to see her through the glass window of the nursery. She watched from her bed as Ann and the doctor looked at her baby through the nursery window and talked as if they had done the whole thing by themselves.

The doctor gave her a pill. "This will dry up your milk." She had wanted to nurse, but was afraid to say anything because they would give her baby away.

After the spinal wore off, Beverly walked to the nursery window and the nurse pointed to her daughter. She asked if she could hold her and was told that it was not feeding time. She walked to the rest room. Depressed because no one would let her hold her baby, Beverly flopped on a wooden stool to wait for the stall to be free. She came right back up, "Man did that hurt!" Later she found that the sits baths helped, but it took days before she sat comfortably again.

Ann told Beverly that she was very pleased that she had named her daughter after Sue. Beverly didn't answer, but thought, *Grandma's name had nothing to do with naming my daughter. Why rock the boat? If it keeps her from hitting me or my daughter, let her think what she wants.*

Beverly finally got to hold her baby. She knew that her daughter was the only person that would ever love her. She felt it when she held her daughter that first time because she smiled as Beverly removed the blanket to look at her fingers and toes. They were perfect with little tiny nails that needed trimmed. She fed her daughter from the bottle and felt complete for the first time. Just then the woman who had shaved her privates walked into the room. She walked to her bed. "I just came to see the brat!"

Beverly's head exploded. *People could do or say anything they want about me, but by God, nobody is going to treat my daughter that way!!* She pushed the call button and told the woman to get out. She told the nurse to call Ann and the doctor. When Ann called, Beverly told her that she was taking her daughter and leaving the hospital if that is the way her daughter was going to be treated. Ann and Ted came to pick them up and the nurse apologized.

When they got home Beverly tried to take care of her daughter the way Ann told her to, but again she could not do anything to please her mother. Ann took over the baby's care and told Beverly that if she tried to take her daughter anywhere without Ann being with her, she would make sure that the baby was adopted out and that Beverly would never see her again.

Beverly resumed praying that her mother would die so she could have her daughter. She knew that Ann would never allow her to be the baby's mother as long as she lived.

Ann took Beverly, the baby and Becky to the Iowa State Fair. Beverly wanted to push the baby's stroller, but Ann told her that she would push it. Beverly resented the fact that she couldn't even push her own daughter's stroller. She told Ann that she was going to the rest room. Not only did she not go back to meet them, she went with the Carnie to Minneapolis and worked the booths.

Carnie wanted to have sex up Beverly's hind end. She remembered what John had done and fought. An old man, probably in his 40s, told her that he had kidnapped her and wouldn't let her out of the hotel room. She knew that she would not win in a fight so she had sex with him until he asked her to leave. She wouldn't leave him alone. It took a couple of days and nights, but he finally opened the door for her.

Beverly walked to the nearest phone and called the police to pick her up. She told them what had happened and they called her parents. Ann and Ted went to Minneapolis, retrieved her and took her home.

Beverly had infection in her tubes so bad that she couldn't stand, sit, or lay comfortably. It took lots of medication to cure it, but she ended up with closed tubes from it. That was probably a blessing because she never had another child.

Ann always could tell when Beverly was in trouble; the exact day and time she needed help. Somehow she was that tuned in to Beverly's emotions when she was gone. Too bad she couldn't have put that gift to better use. Instead, she berated Beverly, shamed her, telling her what a bad person she was. All that did was make Beverly determined to leave again as soon as she got the chance.

Ann's intuition scared Beverly, but when Beverly started feeling the future, it really freaked her out. She was changing her baby's diaper and an overwhelming knowing came over her. "You are going to die," came out of her mouth. Beverly's hands rose as if she had touched a hot stove and the baby smiled at Beverly. Beverly finished putting her diaper on, carried her to the living room, and placed her on the floor in front of Ann. She never touched the baby again.

There was a blizzard one evening. Ted didn't come home on time. The hours dragged on, the weather got worse and Beverly became distraught. She started sobbing and Ann tried to comfort her. She asked, "What is the matter with you?"

Beverly sobbed, "He's dead! I dreamed that somebody in the family died in a car accident, but I couldn't see who it was. It is Dad!"

Ann assured her that she was wrong and a short time later Ted drove into the driveway.

Ann had explained to Beverly what a gentleman was. She said that they treated you nice and didn't want only sex. Beverly doesn't remember where she met her first husband, but she married him a few months after her daughter was born so she could have her daughter live with them and they could be a family.

Her husband was joining the army and Beverly and her baby could join him after he was through boot camp. On their wedding night he kissed her on the cheek, said, "Goodnight Honey," rolled over and went to sleep.

Her only thought was, *Wrong again, Ma! This gentleman crap isn't going to be that great. I like sex, but if I can have my daughter with me, it'll be worth it.*

Her husband left for the Army the next morning and she went back to her parents' farm. Ann was all for her getting married, but she told Beverly that she couldn't take the baby with her. In fact, she moved Beverly into a second floor, one-bedroom apartment in the city.

Beverly was alone, frustrated and started drinking again. It wasn't supposed to be like this. She had a husband and child, but couldn't be with either one. After several months Ann finally came and took her back to the farm.

Beverly was sent through a vocational rehabilitation assessment program to see what type of education she should take. She was sent out of state to attend a business college. That seemed to be Ann's dream for her. She told Beverly over and over that she would be a good secretary because she had long fingers for typing.

The day Beverly left to attend the business college was the last time she saw her baby alive. She was sitting in her high chair with her arms raised, "Mamamama." Beverly knew that she was powerless. She was never going to be allowed to be her baby's mother. She turned and walked out the door.

Ann drove Beverly to a Victorian house in another state where many working women lived. She left her in a room and drove away. Beverly got up the next morning, got on the bus, and went to the business college. There were people there who seemed to know what they were doing. No one talked to her and she felt alone. Little did she know that she was still living with the remnants from the shock treatments and medications she had been forced to take for three years.

Beverly doesn't remember exactly how long she attended classes, but it seems like a couple of days. Her next memory is of drinking in a car with several boys, having sex with them all, and being dropped in the early morning hours in front of the house she was living in.

She was drunk and stumbling. She knocked, but no one answered so she started banging on the window and yelling. One of the windows broke and she cut her hand. The police came and took her to jail because she was at the wrong house. Later that day they carried her around in their squad car to find the house she was in with the boys. Then Ann and Ted came after her and took her back to the farm.

The next day Ann moved Beverly into an efficiency apartment in the city. They talked and Ann told her, "Someday I won't be here. You'll have to learn to live without me." That statement shot through Beverly like electricity because she somehow knew it was vatic.

Ann asked Beverly if she wanted to see her baby. Beverly was so ashamed that she simply couldn't face her daughter. She said, "Not today." Ann said that she would pick her up the next morning so she could go Christmas shopping with her, Becky, and the baby. Ann left to pick up the baby who had stayed with Teddy's family while Ann and Ted picked up Beverly.

Beverly put her clothes away, took a long soaking bath, and fixed a sandwich. She visited with the female neighbor she shared the bathroom with and went to bed early.

Beverly sat straight up in bed the next morning like she'd been shot, but no one was in the room. She didn't see anything out of the ordinary. She got out of bed and turned on the radio. She washed up, got dressed and waited for Ann to arrive. She didn't come.

The news came on the radio. There had been a car accident. Ann had been killed along with...Beverly's brain turned off. She doesn't remember leaving the apartment. The next memory she has is of stumbling on the sidewalk, "NO! NO! NO!" She was stumbling, falling in the snow, and getting up, but didn't know where she was going, just going. She couldn't quit screaming, "NO! NO! NO!"

Somehow she entered the vocational rehabilitation building. A woman asked, "Are you all right?"

Beverly looked at her. "Mom, Becky and my baby are dead..."

She caught Beverly's arm as she broke down sobbing. "You sit here at the table. What makes you say that?"

Beverly finally collected herself and told the woman that she had heard everything on the radio. The woman told Beverly that she would be back and left. When she came back she asked Beverly to call the sheriff to make sure it was actually her family.

Beverly called the sheriff. She knew that the sheriff hated her because he had told her so when he tracked her down, but she thought he would at least tell her that she had heard wrong. When he answered Beverly told him who she was using her maiden name and asked, "Was that my family that was killed in the car accident?"

...The sheriff said, "I thought you got married."

"I did. Was that my family?"

"Well, what is your last name now?"

"Please, was that them?"

"Are you going to answer me?"

"You son-of-a-bitch!" as she slammed the phone back on its receiver.

The woman asked, "Was it them?"

Beverly sobbed, "I don't know. He wouldn't answer me."

Then she had Beverly call the radio station that she had been listening to in order to confirm the names. Beverly made the call. The person confirmed the names and apologized for Beverly hearing them on the radio. She almost collapsed as she hung up.

The woman took Beverly back to a chair and told her that she would be right back. It seemed like an eternity, but when she returned she didn't speak. She took Beverly's elbow and guided her to the car. They drove to the hospital in silence and walked into the main entrance.

Beverly was about to ask the receptionist if her family was there when she felt an arm go around her shoulders that guided her down the hall. It was her doctor. She realized for the first time that it was real. Ann, Becky and her baby were dead.

Shock is a wonderful thing. It protects us from emotional overload. The doctor guided Beverly down the hall to where she saw Teddy and somehow she was guided into Ted's arms. He told Beverly that Becky was being examined in the emergency room.

She sobbed, "She's alive?"

"Yes, but she's in pretty bad shape."

"Mom and my baby?"

Tears came to his eyes and he shook his head.

The doors opened and a cart rolled down the hall and stopped in front of the elevator. Becky was on it. She was gray and looked dead. Ted signed the papers that were handed to him so she could be operated on and she was rolled into the elevator. The doors closed.

Beverly asked Ted, "Will you go to the chapel with me?"

He nodded.

They sat there next to each other in silence. She promised God that if He would let Becky live that she would be the best person she could be. She promised that she would do anything if He would just let her live…please. Somewhere Beverly had heard that even if Becky lived that she would not be able to walk. She begged God for this to not be true.

Becky made it through surgery. Beverly and her family sat in the hall and waited. They took turns going in to see her. She had traction on her left leg. She looked like she was asleep. Beverly would hold her hand and pet it, "It'll be okay. You are going to be all right. You rest now."

Beverly was washing her hands in the rest room. Kim came in. "If Ann would have let us adopt your baby, she wouldn't be dead now!"

Beverly's head exploded, but she knew that Kim was right. She didn't say anything, just dropped deeper into the abyss of depression and hopelessness. She walked back into the hall and sat down. Ted said, "It's your turn, Beverly." She got up and walked into Becky's room.

The nurse told her, "Talk to her and see if you can get her to wake up."

Beverly said, "Come on, Becky, it's time to go to school."

Becky moved, her eyes shot open, and she tried to get out of bed.

Beverly patted her shoulder. "It's okay." She relaxed.

Beverly asked, "Do you know who I am?"

Becky's look was questioning as she nodded.

Beverly asked, "Who am I?"

Becky said, "Beverly."

Beverly told her to go back to sleep and she would see her when she woke up. Becky closed her eyes.

Beverly looked at the nurse. She smiled and nodded her head.

Beverly was sobbing from joy when she walked out of the room, but the family thought something had happened. Finally she was able to say, "She recognized me."

Ted took Beverly to her apartment. The door was standing halfway open. She apparently had not shut it when she left. After she got cleaned up, they went to see the wrecked car that had been towed to a nearby town.

The front seat was bent backwards behind the steering wheel. There was blood on it from Ann and Beverly's baby. Beverly wanted to vomit. She was lightheaded, but wanted to be strong for Ted's sake. Neither of them spoke.

They went to another town to pick out the caskets for Ann and the baby. Ann's was blue and the baby's was pink. Beverly wasn't allowed to pick out the dress that her baby would be buried in. Kim did that. The dress was white.

Beverly told Ted about a dress that Ann had bought. It was too small, but she wanted to loose weight so she could wear it. "Maybe she can finally get into it if they split it in the back?" It seems like that is what Ann was buried in, but Beverly isn't sure.

Ann's engagement ring was very special to her. She told Beverly, over and over, the story about Ted walking over the top of snow drifts from his farm to her house in the city to keep a date with her after a blizzard. He had stayed long enough to get warmed up and then walked home so he could be there to do the chores in the morning. Ann said that her engagement ring only had a diamond chip in it because that was all Ted could afford, but his real gift to her was his devotion, honesty, and steadfastness.

Beverly told Ted that she thought Ann should be buried with her engagement ring. The splice had fallen out and she had quit wearing it for fear of losing it. Ted made sure that it was buried with Ann.

No one was talking to Beverly. She knew that they blamed her for what happened. She knew that it was her fault because she had prayed for Ann to die. God had punished her for all the bad stuff she'd done by killing her baby, too.

The day of the funeral was horrible. John, Mary, Teddy and Kim were there. Neighbors brought food and Beverly was supposed to eat before the funeral, but she was on the verge of throwing up. It was surreal. People were laughing and she didn't see anything funny. Nobody spoke to her and she was grateful for that.

When it was time to get into the limousine that the funeral home provided, Ted pushed Beverly away so Ann's cousin, Jerry, could sit in the front seat with him. Teddy and Kim got into the third seat and John and Mary climbed into the middle one. John acted like Beverly was supposed to sit by him, but she walked around to the other side and sat next to Mary.

The church was packed with people. Beverly didn't hear a word that the minister said. Her knuckles were white from clinching her fists and her ears were buzzing so loud that she couldn't concentrate on anything. Then it was time to walk past the caskets and leave. Beverly kissed Ann's forehead. It was like kissing a cold, hard rock. She approached her baby's casket and broke, "No! No! No!"

The woman from the funeral home grabbed her and slapped her. "Your dad doesn't need you to be stupid! You shut up and get into the car!" as she shoved Beverly down the church steps. Beverly shut down immediately, just like she had been trained to do for so many years.

Beverly climbed into her ascribed seat and sat motionless. She made sure that she didn't cry. Her family was crying as the caskets were carried down the steps. Ann's was placed into the hearse and the baby's was put into the back of a station wagon. Beverly sat there looking at her family, wondering why they were allowed to cry, but she wasn't.

The things Ann had told her about each of them came flooding back. Mary didn't like Beverly and she didn't like having sex with John. *No wonder he is always after me.*

Ann hated Kim because she made Teddy divorce Diane and leave

Sandy. Then he adopted out Sandy and Ann never saw her granddaughter again. Beverly wondered if that bothered Ted who had now lost two granddaughters.

A woman who Beverly had taught Sunday school with walked up to the limousine window. Beverly rolled the window down. The woman held Beverly's hand and said the only thing that made any sense to her that day. "I care, Beverly." She will always appreciate that lady's comment. To this day, that is what Beverly says to people when she doesn't know how to express how bad she feels for them.

Ann and the baby were buried next to each other. Beverly asked Ted if she could have the plot next to her baby and he told her, "No! That's where I'll be buried."

Beverly was more distraught. She wasn't going to be able to be with her baby, even in death.

Ted took Beverly to her apartment and drove away.

CHAPTER 2

Beverly went to the hospital several times to see Becky while she was recovering from the accident. Becky's left hip had been badly damaged and was ultimately fused, her left thigh bone had to have several screws to hold it together, both of her arms were broken and healed well, her spleen was removed, and her other injuries also healed. Ted told Beverly, "The doctor said if she lives she will not walk again, but don't tell her."

There was a baby in the crib next to Becky. It had a growth on its back that was hard to look at. Besides, Beverly didn't want to be around babies at that moment. She had tried to pick up one of Teddy's children, but Kim grabbed it out of her arms just as the empty space her baby left when she died started feeling occupied. She never tried to hold one of them again.

Everybody was taking Becky gifts and flowers in the hospital. Beverly didn't have a job or any money. She felt ashamed that she couldn't show Becky how much she wanted her to be all right, but she didn't know how to say so. Beverly didn't go back after Becky wanted her to bring her a big teddy bear. She just couldn't face Becky's disappointment.

Beverly sat in her apartment for a few days trying to cope with everything. She doesn't remember how long, but finally she called a cab to take her to a bar. She remembers telling him that her daughter and mother were killed in a car accident. She remembers looking at him and wanting him to tell her that she was wrong. That it didn't happen. Instead, he told her how sorry he was to hear her story and cashed her check for an extra ten dollars.

That started Beverly writing bad checks. She didn't have any money in her checking account, none of the family ever came to see if she was all right, and she slipped from depression into perdition. She drank, shot, and popped anything she could get her hands on to kill the pain.

In the next month or so she told her story to many cabdrivers and bartenders. They always cashed her checks for an extra ten dollars. None of them ever told her what she wanted to hear, "You're wrong! Your daughter and mother are at home waiting to hear from you."

Men paid Beverly to have sex with them. Twenty dollars was her usual charge for whatever they wanted. Once in a while one would pay her $100 to stay all night. She refused the really kinky stuff like stuffing a potato up her rear; however, sucking her toes while they jacked off was all right for forty dollars.

One morning there was a knock on Beverly's door. There were two men standing there. She recognized one of them. He was on the vice squad. He and his partner came into the key clubs often when she was drinking, but she didn't recognize the other man.

Beverly opened the door and asked them to come in. The man she didn't recognize introduced himself as some kind of investigator for the Army. It seems that her husband had committed bigamy three times. The investigator wanted her to sign papers that she was still married to him. She told him that as far as she knew they were, but she hadn't been in contact with him for months.

Everything was going fine until he asked her for her birthdate. She told him. Seconds passed before the vice officer exclaimed, "Seventeen?" Beverly smiled sheepishly at him and nodded. At the time, twenty-one was the drinking age.

Beverly signed the papers and she never saw the investigator again; however, every time she tried to go into a key club after that, the vice squad picked her up and took her to jail for drinking under age. She thinks she was picked up once for prostitution, but they couldn't prove it so she was released.

Things got pretty bizarre. Beverly was drinking all of the alcohol, shooting nose inhalers and popping all of the pills she could get her hands on. She wanted to join her daughter, but was too scared to be direct.

Beverly bought a used car with a check and had new tires put on it with another one. She put gas in it at a rural country store and got some extra cash for beer. She bought clothes that didn't fit with checks so she could get cash.

Everybody in the family was busy with Becky. Beverly felt alone. She blamed herself for her daughter and mother's deaths. After all, hadn't she prayed that Ann would die and leave her alone with her daughter? Hadn't Ann told Beverly the day before her death, "Someday I'll be gone and you'll have to take care of yourself."

Beverly drove a man and woman to Kansas City. She doesn't remember why? She was taking some kind of uppers along with the gallons of beer every day, trying to kill the pain. She doesn't remember starting back alone, but remembers awareness returning as she was driving across a bridge and a semi just missed her going the opposite direction. She was so high that she wasn't scared, but realized that she didn't know where she was. She stopped at the next filling station and asked the attendant. She was a few miles from the city.

It occurred to Beverly that it would be easier for the cops to find her if she kept the car. After all, she didn't know how many checks she had written, several books. She decided that she had to ditch the car. She drove to a gravel road and followed it to a small river. She pointed the car at the ditch, opened the door and put her left foot on the ground, gunned the motor with her right foot, slipped the converted automatic transmission into drive, and stepped out of the car. It went down the bank and disappeared into the brush. She felt nothing.

Beverly started walking down the road. A fuel truck picked her up and she thought she had gotten away with discarding the car, but a sheriff's car appeared and the truck driver stopped. Apparently, a farmer's wife had been looking out the window and called the police when she saw a car go into the river.

The deputy made his call to the station and took Beverly into custody for bad checks. He put her in the back seat of his car and took her to jail. She used her one phone call to contact Ted. She told him where she was and why. He said, "You got yourself into it. Get yourself out of it," and hung up.

Did Ted know that Beverly had been praying for Ann to die? All she knew for sure is that Ted blamed her, too. She remembers relaxing the same way she did for Ann when she beat her or when John hurt her. "Okay God, kill me if you want to! I deserve it!"

Beverly was transferred to the county jail to await her trial. There were six sets of bunks in the interior cell with a walkway around the bars. It had a partitioned off bathroom. The women in jail were a lot different than in the mental wards. They were meaner, more boisterous, and many were black. Most everybody was white in Beverly's hometown and she had never been around black people. Their mannerisms scared her. She wanted OUT!

A black woman who said she was a prostitute and drug addict told Beverly not to accept any cigarettes from anyone when she got to prison because that person would own and rape her.

How in the heck was a woman going to rape me? Beverly thought, *They don't have a thing!*

Beverly was only there a couple days before she found herself throwing metal pans of peaches and sandwiches at the guard. She was taken to the psychiatric ward and locked in a room. Later a nurse took her to a different room and a doctor said he was going to examine her. Everything was going all right until he wanted to stick his finger up her rectum. She went ballistic. "What is it that everybody wants to stick things up my butt? Doesn't anyone understand that it hurts?" She doesn't remember which of them won that battle, but she assumes that he did.

In a few days Beverly was allowed to wander the ward with the other patients. She caused no problems. She had been in mental wards off and on for several years and understood the rules. She wasn't interested in learning the rules of jail…thank you.

A few days later, Beverly was taken to court in a different county. She doesn't remember much about it except her court-appointed attorney told the judge that she plead guilty. He didn't talk to her before she went before the judge and she didn't know that she could plead anything but guilty. Nobody told her that she could plead not guilty and ask that the circumstances of her daughter and mother's deaths be taken into account. She was a 17-year-old farmer's kid. She had just been through the worst mental and emotional trauma of her life. What did she know?

Beverly knew that the county sheriff hated her because he told her every time he found her after she had run away from home. Ann had told her that two county sheriffs had told her to lock Beverly up and forget she ever had her. Both had chased Beverly down every time she ran away. Of course, Ann also told Beverly that she would kill her if she ever told anyone about what she and John had done. It never occurred to Beverly that she could say anything.

Beverly had never told anyone and didn't think anyone would believe her now. Besides, what difference did it make now? Her baby was dead and she could never be her mother. Ted wasn't even going to let her be buried next to her baby.

Beverly was taken back to the county jail instead of the mental ward. This time they took her to the cell next to the one she had been in the first time. It was a mirror image, except the bathroom was much smaller.

This time Beverly filled the bathtub with water, told the black woman in the bunk next to the bathroom door that she was going to kill herself, and submerged her head in the water. She must have looked like an idiot standing on the floor with her head in the water, but it worked. The black woman grabbed Beverly.

Beverly reacted with her left arm, and the woman flew into her bunk and hit her head. The next thing Beverly knew she was being taken back to the mental ward.

Beverly turned eighteen on that mental ward, nine days later her court-appointed attorney entered a guilty plead on her behalf for false uttering. The judge sentenced her to, "Seven years at hard labor."

From Beverly's perspective, bad things just seemed to keep happening to her and she had no control over any of it. She could fight, flee, or relax and try to survive. That's what she did. She just relaxed.

Beverly remembers looking at the fields on the trip to the women's reformatory. She didn't know anything about prisons, but she sure didn't like the jail she had been in.

The woman in the back seat with Beverly and the driver made small talk, but Beverly didn't remember saying anything. There wasn't anything to say. Her family hated her, she hated her, and she was on her way to "seven years at hard labor."

As the car hummed down the road Beverly remembered seeing something on TV about prisoners pounding on rocks with sledge hammers. Weren't they trying to break them into smaller rocks? Another question came to her, "What do they do with the rocks after we break them up?" She just knew that there would be a rock pile that she would be standing on with a sledge hammer for seven years, breaking big rocks into small ones. She thought, *You don't suppose that's where they get those really little rocks they put on roads do you? That WILL take years to do!*

They finally arrived at the women's reformatory. There was a tree-lined, winding driveway that ended at big white stucco buildings with red tile roofs. There was a walkway with a lot of arches connecting three of the buildings and a circular driveway around a grassy circle with a flag pole in the middle. Large trees shaded the buildings on the west. Beverly thought, *This doesn't look that bad. Where's the wall? I know I saw a wall on the TV!*

Beverly was taken to the medical room where a mean-looking old woman said she was the nurse. An even older man claimed to be the doctor. Her clothes were taken away and she was examined. The only time she raised a fuss was when he tried to finger her anus. Then they had problems.

With that over and them winning, she was taken to a small

bathroom. She didn't even say anything when a different woman sprayed her with bug spray in the shower, "I'm a prisoner, too." she said. "This is my detail. They make me spray everybody that comes in. Some women come in with lice, crabs, or something. They don't want all of us to catch anything."

Beverly thought, *I had crabs once. Mom didn't believe me when I told her that I must have gotten them off the stool.* Then again, the doctor had told Ann that crabs come from sexual contact. Beverly cringed and thought, "I don't want them again, bugs crawling around all over my privates was one of the most miserable feelings I ever had. It was worth the beating to get the medicine that killed them."

The other prisoner was pleasant enough. Beverly watched her having her own conversation. It filled in the time. "You'll go to isolation for a month and then get your own room and detail. Where you from?"

Beverly told her.

"Whacha in for?"

"Checks."

She gave Beverly an ugly blue dress with snaps from her belly button up to the collar to put on over cotton panties and bra, then white tube socks and heavy brown shoes with brown laces. She received a pile of linens. The prisoner asked if Beverly smoked. She said yes and was handed an ashtray, a book of matches, a funny red metal device with a brown strap and a package that said Bugler tobacco. Then she was directed out the door.

Women in the same blue dresses and gray pant uniforms gawked at Beverly as she was paraded down the wide hall, up the steps, to the end of that hall and into the room. After she entered, the heavy wood door slammed closed. She turned quickly to see that the only opening was a wire transom above the door. There was no handle on the door. She hadn't liked the clang of steel doors closing when she was in jail, but this was a different sound, more ominous, more permanent.

Beverly turned back to the room. There was a single bed by the heat radiator and window. Large curved metal tubes with smaller vertical tubes in the middle served as the head and foot boards. The pillow was flat, the mattress was lumpy, and the room was cold. The window consisted of four vertical rows of small panes. Each was surrounded by metal. The side panels opened, but were too small for her head to fit through. Outside was a street and large trees. A sidewalk connected the building to the street.

There was a partition in the corner by the door that housed a white stool and sink. There was a mirror above the wooden table that hugged the south wall. A wooden chair completed the furnishings. The plastered walls and shiny poured-concrete floor were cold.

Beverly laid the linens on the bed and turned the knob on the radiator for heat, wrapped up in the blanket, sat on the bed with her knees to her chest, and rocked back and forth. She didn't cry. She had forgotten how.

Now what, she thought. The woman said that she would be in isolation for a month. *Okay, but what am I supposed to do? I don't know*.

Beverly looked out the window again to see if she could see the rock pile, but couldn't. Finally she decided to make her bed and hang the towels in the half bath. She sat down at the table with the package of tobacco with white papers and the red metal device. "How the hell do I get this to be cigarettes?" she said out loud, "Sure wish I would have learned to roll that pot!"

A woman's voice came from outside the door, "Hi! I'm Donna. Do you smoke?"

"Yeah," Beverly answered, "but I don't know how to make this thing work."

"Just a minute."

Everything was silent and then she heard someone outside the door again. Cigarettes slid under her door, "These will keep you going until tonight when I can show you how the roller works." Everything was silent again.

Beverly remembered what the black prostitute had said in jail about not accepting cigarettes from anybody because they would own her, but that woman had sounded friendly and Beverly sure needed a cigarette. She pulled them from under the door and made a pile on the table. She doesn't remember how many there were, but she knew she could get through until evening.

Beverly sat looking into the mirror. She didn't know the person looking back at her. She had dark circles under her eyes. No makeup. There was no sparkle in those eyes. No life.

Beverly's mind went back through the last year. So much had happened. There was nothing left. Either her family was dead or they wanted nothing to do with her. She had no friends.

Beverly had fought depression for years, but she didn't have any kind of chemical to lessen the depths of blackness that enveloped her as she sat there looking at what was left of eighteen years of socialization by her family.

That evening the meal was served to Beverly in her room by the matron, the woman who had provided her with cigarettes, and another woman that said she worked in the kitchen. The matron allowed Donna to show her how to operate the cigarette roller. Donna happily told Beverly while she was manipulating the tobacco and paper, "You came on a good day! We get popcorn and fudge tonight. You won't be able to watch TV with us, but we'll bring you the goodies!" Beverly politely thanked them and was grateful when the door was closed.

Beverly was in shock! Donna looked more like a man than most men she had sexual intercourse with. Beverly dropped to the floor and gasped, "My God, she owns me now that I accepted cigarettes from her." The thoughts were rampant. *How will she be able to rape me? Who can I tell? There was no one! What will I do? Can I whip her? She isn't as tall as I am. I sure as hell will give it a try!!*

Beverly finally composed herself long enough to eat some of the food that was, by this time, cold. The dishes were picked up. Later that evening, as promised, she got popcorn and fudge. Donna and others talked to her through the door. They told her to slide the table over to the door so she could stand on it and see through the transom while they talked. She was relieved to see that the other prisoners looked like women.

After all the doors were locked, Beverly decided that apparently being raped by a woman didn't hurt like it did when men raped her. The other women didn't seem raped or hurt, and they were laughing with Donna. They didn't seem to be scared.

The next morning was even more horrifying. After the breakfast dishes had been taken away, Beverly heard a tractor stop in the street outside her window. She crawled on the bed and looked out the window. There was Donna with a man. They were carrying a metal tub of food into the building below her. Donna was yelling something toward her window. Beverly opened it to hear, "This is Pat!" Beverly forced a smile and wave, slammed the window closed, fell on her side, clutched her pillow with her knees to her chest, and sobbed, "My God! There are more of them!"

Beverly doesn't know how long she stayed there. It seemed that she was awakened for lunch by Donna telling her that Pat said hello. By this time the only thing Beverly wanted to know was where the rock pile and sledgehammer were.

Donna laughed. "We don't have those here! We farm, garden, and make uniforms." Beverly was real disappointed that she wasn't going to get a sledgehammer.

Isolation was just that, isolation. Women would ask Beverly questions through the door and tell her about themselves, she took test after test and lied to psychologists, but mostly she looked in the mirror. She made a drawing of herself with bottles of booze, pill bottles, needles, guns, and knives around her face. She gave it to one of the matrons. She assumed one of the psychologists would interpret it and put it into her file. She didn't care. Seven years seemed like a long time to her, especially when she had women owning her. Her biggest fear is that she didn't know what was meant by someone owning her.

Beverly was finally let out of that room. Her isolation was over. She didn't have any kind of disease or bugs. That meant that she had to start living with this diverse bunch of women. In case you can't tell, she wanted to stay right where she was for seven years, protected from them.

Beverly was taken to the next building. They called it number one. She was shown to her room. She made her bed, hung up her towels, put away her institutional clothing and was allowed to wander the building. She went to the living room area. They called it "the bay." There was an old, fat woman sitting in one of the chairs. She introduced herself and told Beverly to have a seat.

The woman asked Beverly what she was in for and Beverly told her checks. The woman told Beverly that she and her husband had taken out a life insurance policy on their 12-year-old son, tied him to the bed, set the house on fire, and stood outside listening to him scream while he burned to death.

Beverly just looked at her. She couldn't move or say anything. The woman showed absolutely no remorse. Beverly was sure that there would be a day that the old woman regretted telling her about it that way. Nobody should tell a person who has just lost their child that they killed theirs.

The old woman continued that her husband had died in prison. "But I'm gonna get a pardon someday."

Beverly doesn't remember saying anything. Somehow she found her way back into her room, closed the door, and locked herself in. The matron threatened to lock her up if she didn't come out of her room for lunch. That was all right with her.

One of the older prisoners came into her room and assured her that she would be safe eating lunch. Beverly went with her and kept her fork handy in case she needed to stab somebody. She stayed in her room that afternoon and ate supper with caution. She forewent watching TV, took a shower, and locked herself in her room for the night.

The next morning brought more terror. Beverly was taken to the storeroom in the industrial building. The woman running it told her that she would be working with Donna and Pat. Beverly tried to not look horrified and stayed close the employee. She followed her around like a puppy on a leash. Finally, the employee sent Beverly to the back storeroom that had been used for canning vegetables from the garden. It had several old refrigerated units that no longer worked and one extremely large, walk-in refrigerator.

Pat walked through the door. Beverly started screaming, "NO! NO! NO!" She kept the long metal table between them. She continued screaming and moved the opposite direction as the other woman tried to catch her.

Pat screamed, "STOP! What the hell is the matter with you?"

Beverly blubbered through her sobs about the black prostitute telling her in jail that if she accepted cigarettes from women like her, they would rape her. “Donna gave me cigarettes when I was in isolation. I didn’t know how to run the roller. I’ll pay them back…please don’t rape me!”

Pat looked shocked. Then started laughing, leaned on the table and howled, “You aren’t my type! We just want you to do your share of work. You’re killing us by not carrying your share of the load!”

Beverly started calming down. “You have a type?”

“Yup.”

“You don’t own and rape everybody that you give cigarettes to?”

“Nope…Come on, we got work to do.”

The employee and Donna were standing in the doorway looking at them. Donna asked, “What’s going on?”

“Nothing. Let’s get to work.”

The three worked together as a team after that. Pat and Donna taught Beverly about their views on lesbianism. Donna had been in and out of the reformatory many times and didn’t like life on the outside. Pat was just doing her time and would not come back after she was released. They both preferred sexual relationships with women and Beverly wasn’t their type. She was to pay them back for the cigarettes by making sure that new prisoners had cigarettes and knew how to use the cigarette rollers.

The matrons were old women, 40s or 50s, from the nearby town. They called the prisoners “girls” and treated them the same way. Beverly still doesn’t particularly like it when someone calls her a girl.

Beverly doesn’t remember exactly why she was moved to Building 2, but as soon as she got moved into her room a cottage check happened. That’s where the matron rings a school bell and all inmates have to report to the bay area. The matron and trustees go through each person’s room for contraband.

Beverly was shocked when the staff came to the bay and told her that she was to be put into lockup for having a can of nutmeg in her room. She tried to tell them that it wasn’t hers, but nobody would listen. She didn’t go easy and ended up in the cells on the top floor of the industrial building.

There was a sink and stool on the east wall of her cell. Beverly lay on one flimsy, stained mattress and covered with another one. To get a drink of water she had to lie on her stomach and suck on a straw poked between the bars from the hall. These weren't just bars. They had slats of steel between the bars. If she remembers correctly, there was chicken wire in the frosted glass of the windows across the hall. There were no blinds and the sun beat in during the afternoon.

After Beverly was released from that farce, she had just gotten back to the cottage and something else, she doesn't remember what, was planted in her room during another cottage check. Again, she tried to tell them she had done nothing wrong, but she was locked in the lockup room of the same building this time. It was dark, the windows were darkened, and the door was wood with a square section that could be opened from the outside so they could see what she was doing.

By this time Beverly was fuming. She had an enemy and didn't know who. She knew she was going to complete the punishment, but somebody was going to pay attention when she got out!

Cigarettes and matches were slid under the door during this internment. Other prisoners talked to Beverly and tried to keep her spirits up, but they wouldn't tell her who had planted the items in her room. It would be years before the culprit admitted to her that they had discarded the forbidden items in her room. "You were new and the easiest mark."

Beverly wasn't having a good time! She went silent in that dungeon, determined that this crap was going to stop. She was finally released. The next morning she waited patiently for the matron to unlock the outside cottage door and the superintendent to emerge from her house. After the old woman that the prisoners called "ol' three hairs" went into the administration building, Beverly walked from building two into the administration building. She bypassed the secretary and opened the hall door into the superintendent's office. She told the superintendent, "If you don't quit locking me up for things I haven't done, I'm going to knock your institution down around you, brick by brick!"

The startled old woman looked at her in shock, regained her composure and asked Beverly to take a seat. Beverly didn't realize that the superintendent was apparently familiar with her past experiences of mental hospitals and shock treatments. The old woman tried to be calm and finally asked Beverly to go back to her room. She went. Apparently the old woman took Beverly at her word because later that day she was transferred to a state mental hospital.

Originally, Beverly was locked on the isolation ward where she was observed, counseled, and evaluated. Same old thing, tests and they wanted to examine her rectum and take her temperature the same way. Did Freud teach them that? Is her behind somehow connected to her temper? Could be! They probably thought so! Of course, they won and Beverly finally complied. She knew the rules of mental hospitals. She knew that all she had to do is behave and she would be transferred to an open ward. She did and she was.

Beverly's detail was catching sheets from the huge mangle in the laundry. She didn't particularly like the job. It was summer by then and the mangle was hot, but it was better than being on the locked ward or in prison.

One day Beverly was told to leave work and go to the receptionist's desk in the administration building. She walked to the desk. The receptionist smiled and pointed behind her. Beverly turned around to see Ted and Becky walking toward her. She had given up ever seeing them again. Becky was walking by herself. She wasn't supposed to ever be able to walk again, but she was.

Beverly started crying. They embraced and they all cried. Beverly is not sure that she felt anything except gratitude that Becky could walk. Beverly thought, *Maybe those prayers in the hospital helped then?*

They walked around the grounds and played miniature golf. Beverly knew that they had only come out of obligation. After all, Ted had told her to get herself out of it. There was nothing Beverly could contribute to Becky's life. She was relieved when they left so she could get back to being crazy.

Beverly started going to the apple orchard shortly after that. She could get all of the beer she wanted and there were men there to service her sexually. She went to dances and met a truck driver. They danced to Blue Moon and other slow songs. They met in the tunnel and made out. After he left she met a man from town. He had shot himself in the shoulder. They snuck out one night and met a man with a car. They rode around, drank shots and beer until Beverly was in twilight. All of a sudden red lights were flashing and sirens were blaring. The next thing she knew she was in a wheelchair in an elevator.

It's hazy, but Beverly remembers being moved from the wheelchair into a bed. Then the people left the room and the door closed and was locked. She dropped into oblivion.

Beverly woke because she had to go to the restroom real bad. She staggered to the door, but it was locked. She knocked quietly at first, but when nobody came, she got real loud. The woman who finally came to the door told her to go back to sleep, "It's the middle of the night! Shut up!"

"I have to go to the bathroom real bad!"

"I don't care, you drunk bitch!"

Beverly pounded harder and the woman unlocked the door. She grabbed Beverly by the arm and pushed her down the hall to the bathroom. Beverly didn't fight her because she was going to be able to use a stool instead of peeing all over herself and the floor. The woman shoved her around and used vulgarity to and from the rest room, threatened her about making any more noise, then closed and locked the door.

The next morning Beverly was awakened by staff. She had a horrible hangover. They allowed her to use the restroom. Her clothes had been transferred to her from the prior ward so she cleaned up and changed clothes.

Funny, Beverly doesn't remember where her clothes came from. She wasn't wearing uniforms from prison. Maybe Ted and Becky brought her some from home. Maybe the mental hospital had a clothes closet. She just doesn't remember.

Beverly doesn't remember eating anything that morning, but does remember being given her cigarettes and told where the smoking room was. There was a contraption on the wall by the nurse's station with a wire that got red. She lit her cigarette on it and walked down the hall where a lot of women were tied in large wooden rockers.

The smoking room was larger than Beverly's room and had numerous large wooden rockers. She had been told that morning that she was on the violent ward, so she sat directly across from the doorway with her back to the wall. She wanted to keep an eye out for other patients trying to harm her. All of a sudden the other patients started screaming. Beverly had never heard such a terrifying, horrifying screech. Later she started calling it the Thorazine alarm.

She just appeared in the doorway. She filled the rocker she was tied to. It was hiked up behind her. Her eyes were dark and cold. Beverly just knew she was going to be killed. The huge woman leaped at Beverly, grabbed her lit cigarette, put it in her mouth, and sat the rocker on the floor. She started chewing and rocking in front of Beverly. She chewed with determination as if the cherry hadn't burned her.

Beverly's mouth gaped as the staff ran into the room, grabbed the woman by the arms, and tried to get the cigarette out of her mouth. After she bit them a few times, they gave that idea up, untied her, and dragged her to the end of the hall and into a room. Beverly was still in shock as she stood in the hall watching the fight to get the woman into the room.

Later, Beverly learned there was a restraint bed in that room where unruly patients were tied down. She watched more than one patient slapped around when they wouldn't calm down and shut up fast enough for the staff. Beverly begged the staff to not hurt her fellows, but was told, "You shut your fucking mouth if you don't want to join her!"

Beverly spent about a month on that locked ward. She taught the cigarette woman to walk into the smoking room and ask for a cigarette. The second morning when the Thorazine alarm went off, Beverly jumped beside the door and slammed the rocker to the floor as the woman entered. Then she handed her an unlit cigarette. Beverly talked the staff into allowing her to stay there. Beverly talked to the woman about the outside world. The third morning the woman stopped and peaked around the door. Beverly smiled and handed her an unlit cigarette. She smiled, put it in her mouth, walked over to Beverly's rocker, put hers on the floor beside it, and looked at her. Beverly took the look to mean, *Are you going to talk to me today?* She did.

A few days later, Beverly was allowed to go to the cafeteria and eat her meals with the other patients. They walked single file to and from the cafeteria. The woman in front of Beverly had menstrual blood on the back of her dress. She told one of the staff who said that she didn't care and if Beverly wanted to continue eating in the cafeteria, "You'll shut up!"

Beverly watched the other patient while she ate her lunch. She didn't say anything and didn't use utensils. She focused on her food and ate like an animal. Beverly asked a different staff member about the patient when they got back to the ward. They said that her name was Beverly, she had witnessed one of her parents kill the other and then commit suicide when she was young. She had been institutionalized for many years. "I've never heard her talk. She grunts when she wants something."

Beverly asked if she could help the woman clean up and put a pad on. The staff told her, "If you want to."

Beverly walked over to her namesake and told her why she needed to clean up. "I'll help you if you want me to." The patient looked away so Beverly told her, "I'll be in the smoking room if you change your mind." Beverly sat in the smoking room, talking to the cigarette woman most of the afternoon. Finally, the other patient came to the doorway. Beverly asked, "Would you like me to help you now?"

She looked in a questioning matter.

Beverly got up, walked past her, down the hall and into the large bathroom. She came in while Beverly was drawing the bath water. The staff was apparently watching because one of them brought clean clothes and a pad for her. Beverly helped the woman undress and get into the tub. She washed her back gently and watched while the woman washed. Beverly told her how proud she was that she decided to let her help. "Do you know that my name is Beverly, too? Just like your name."

This patient joined the other one in the smoking room for Beverly's daily rambling about the outside world. She told them about rain washing over her face and how sleet and snow hurt in high winds. She talked about grass between her toes on a warm spring day and how much fun wading in mud is. She didn't talk about politics or religion, just different feelings and emotions. She talked about how nice it would be if everyone treated everybody else the way they wanted to be treated.

The day came that Beverly was transferred back to the prison. She was almost to the locked door when she heard somebody softly say, "Beverly?" She turned around. It was Beverly. A lump came to her throat and tears filled her eyes. They looked deep into each others eyes. Beverly knew that the patient's life wouldn't be the same and so did she. Beverly whispered, "I'll be back." She dropped her head, turned and left.

Forty years later, Beverly went back as an investigator for an advocacy agency. Beverly wasn't there. She has no idea what happened to her. She can only pray that she was one of the women who was rehabilitated during the 1960s and '70s and found happiness in a life that started with such trauma.

For the first time Beverly was looking forward to returning to prison. It was becoming easier to walk away from people that mattered to her. Apparently nothing lasted very long.

Beverly was given permission to go to the basement of the chapel so she could cry through the clarinet and saxophone. That seemed to be the only way she could expel her pain and sadness. It was there that she was finally able to start healing from the death of her baby and the hatred of Ann and John.

Beverly doesn't remember what her detail was after she returned to prison, but she went in front of the parole board shortly afterwards. A woman on the panel told her, "If you ever want to leave here, you will join AA." Beverly was shocked. She couldn't say anything, but thought to herself, *What does she mean ever? I only have seven years!* Needless to say, Beverly asked the matron, "Can I join AA, whatever that is."

Beverly learned that AA meant Alcoholics Anonymous. She was given a blue book with that name on the front of it. *Well*, she thought, *I will read this so I can play the game and get the hell out of here.* She read it.

The problem with reading it was that she could finally answer the question Ted had yelled at her numerous times, "What the hell is wrong with you?" She never knew what to say. Ann told her that she couldn't tell him what John had done. Besides, why tell him that Ann beat her? He knew it. He'd dragged her off of Beverly with, "You're going to kill her, Ann!"

Now Beverly knew how to answer Ted after reading the book. "I'm an alcoholic."

An older woman who had a life sentence for murder took Beverly under her wing. They went to institutional AA meetings where people, mainly men, came into the facility and taught them how to stay sober. She was Beverly's sponsor. They talked. She taught Beverly how to deal with the other women, stay out of trouble, mind her own business and do her own time.

One morning, Beverly awoke to find that her sponsor had died during the night.

Beverly was walking on the sidewalk to the chapel that morning when the hearse drove out the driveway. She watched it go between the two rows of trees. She told her dead sponsor, "You are free now! God bless you!…Thank you!"

All of a sudden Beverly started crying. She couldn't quit. She was almost doubled over as all of the ignored pain broke loose. Beverly finally got to the basement of the chapel. She was on the floor, knees to her chest. Her stomach had knives grinding back and forth. She rolled back and forth blubbering. She had never experienced such emptiness, such excruciating loss as all of the cumulative pain enveloped her.

Beverly doesn't know how long she was there. She was weak by the time she could finally stop crying. She rolled on her side and lay there while the pain retreated to bearable again. She didn't play her beloved instruments that day. She couldn't.

Beverly made up her mind that she would continue going to AA, read the Big Book, and do what it said. Her sponsor had taught her that she was worthwhile and there was a way for her to live a fulfilling life. Beverly believed her. She was mad at God, but her sponsor told her that it would be all right. "He can handle it!"

The country stopped in 1963, so did the inmates. Time seemed to stand still as they gathered in the bay and watched JFK being shot time after time. Beverly didn't know why she was crying, but she joined everyone else. She suspects that she felt safe doing so for the first time in her life.

Beverly was dining room girl so she could have time to attend typing, short hand, etcetera, classes. She set up the tables for meals and tore them down. She remembers walking on the sidewalk to the cottage after class when another prisoner told her that JFK had been shot. She laughed at her and said something like, "Yeah, VERY FUNNY!" Beverly probably could walk to that spot on the sidewalk today. It is that galvanized in her memory.

The inmates and staff got over JFK's death like the rest of the country. They watched people being beaten on TV who were trying to desegregate flags and people who were against the war in Viet Nam. Prison seemed to Beverly to be a pretty safe place by that time. She learned early that "mean" is afraid of "crazy" and everyone pretty much left her alone since she had been a mental patient.

Beverly talked to the psychologists that came to the facility from a university. She started going to chapel with the Catholics. She liked the ceremonial feeling about God. They got on their knees to pray. She didn't feel that in her church growing up. She didn't understand the Latin, but they gave her a booklet to translate it. She even counseled with the priest and told him that she had lied about her brother not being married. She thought that her conversation was privileged like it was with the psychologists, but found out later that he contacted her brother's priest. She figured that was one of the reasons her brother wanted nothing to do with her, but she still didn't understand why the original priest had believed a small child in the first place.

By the time that she was allowed to leave on parole, she believed that she could stay sober with the help of God and AA. She had served seventeen and one half months on her seven year sentence. She walked out of prison with hope in her heart that her life would get better.

Beverly went back to her father's farm to do her parole. The first Sunday was a family dinner to supposedly welcome her home. Her grandparents, brother, his wife and kids joined Ted and Becky. Beverly was nervous because she wasn't used to being around anyone but convicts. She watched her language, used the manners Ann had taught her, and got through the meal. She went to her room after the dishes were finished.

Becky had taken over the bedroom with the desk and Beverly was relegated back to her original room. She was relaxing on the bed when Kim walked up the steps and sat on her bed, "I just want you to know that I don't believe what Grandma said."

Beverly had no idea what she was talking about. "What did Grandma say?"

"She said that you were just coming home to take Dad for everything he has."

Beverly didn't say anything. There wasn't anything to say. The pain pierced her essence as she knew it was intended to do. She finally told Kim to leave after she had babbled on in her maraud.

Beverly asked Ted about it after everyone left. He didn't deny it. He just told her, "Don't worry about it."

The only AA meeting that Beverly's parole officer told her about was in the city. She walked into the cafeteria where it was held. The men were in suits and all of the women seemed to be dressed in diamonds and furs. Beverly knew that she stood out like a sore thumb with her homemade clothing, but was determined to go to AA.

An old man greeted her with a hand shake and welcomed her. It was a speaker's meeting. Beverly had always had discussion meetings in prison. She rather enjoyed being able to just listen and not have to say anything, but she knew that she didn't belong there. She needed to find people like her that knew what it was like to struggle.

Later that week Beverly found a downtown AA group. Ted drove

Beverly to the downtown AA meeting. A nice man told Ted that he would drive Beverly the thirty miles home after the meeting. Ted asked Beverly, "Will that be all right? Tomorrow is a school day and Becky can get some sleep." Beverly agreed to the offer and watched them drive away.

Beverly and the man climbed the steps to the room where AA was held. The people were more like her. They were dressed casually and swore when they spoke. She was relieved when they told her that it was a discussion meeting. She identified with these people when they talked because she didn't know how to live "outside" without drinking. Neither did they, but they were doing it.

They told how they stood still and hurt rather than going to the bar to get rid of the pain. They talked about being nice to people when they wanted to knock the shit out of them. They said that sometimes they had to say the Serenity Prayer over and over, but they didn't have to go to jail when they worked the program.

Beverly was happy as she and the man walked back down the steps after the meeting. She had finally found people that could help her survive; stay sober without going to jail or back to prison. He opened her car door, she got in, he closed the door, walked around the car and got in. He looked at her, "Well, you ready to go have a beer?"

Beverly's head exploded with, *You lying motherfuckers! I believed you! What is the use?* She said, "Yeah."

Beverly didn't understand that some people go to those meetings to prey on vulnerable people who are trying to find sobriety, happiness, and peace.

That was Beverly's demise. All hope for sobriety was gone. She was drunk before he took her home. That same week two lesbians that she had done time with called her. They came from the outskirts of Iowa to party with her in the city. She ended up moving with them to the outskirts of Iowa, but when they figured out that she wanted to date men, they threw her out. She got drunk and ended up in jail where a jailer raped her during the night. She knew better than say anything. Who would believe an ex-con?

Beverly went back to Ted's farm after she was released from jail for being a vagrant. She got to ride the train for the first time because Ted sent her money for the ticket. She sat next to a Catholic nun. Her clothing intimidated Beverly at first, but as they talked and Beverly figured out that the nun was pretty much a human being instead of some kind of saint, she relaxed and enjoyed the trip.

Beverly got a job at a nursing home in a neighboring town. Ted bought her a car and she worked 7:00 am to 3:00 pm so she could be home when Becky got home from school.

Most days she would have a glass of beer while she fixed supper and Becky would have a glass of pop. Beverly would listen to Becky's problems and tell her that everything was going to be all right, even when she didn't believe it herself. She wanted Becky to be all right and not end up like her.

One day Becky came home from school and went directly to her room. Beverly thought about going up and asking what was wrong, but she had learned to give people their space in prison and waited for her to come down to talk.

A few minutes before Ted was to come home, Becky walked into the kitchen and sat down at the table. Beverly got her a glass of pop, a beer for herself, and sat across the table. Beverly was taking a drink when Becky asked, "What's fucking?"

Beverly fought the urge to exhale the beer into the air, concentrated on swallowing, and thought, *What would Mom say?...No!* She said, "You know what sexual intercourse is?"

"Ya?"

"Well, fucking is like cussing. It's just a nasty way of talking about something that is beautiful."

Beverly took another drink and Becky asked, "Doesn't it hurt?"

Again Beverly had to concentrate on swallowing. "No, not when you love the person."

Beverly looked at Becky to see if it was safe to take another drink. As she tipped the glass, Becky asked, "Beverly, did you love 'em all?"

The beer came out her nose that time, "Yes, Becky, at the time I thought I did," as she grabbed a towel to wipe up the mess.

That seemed to satisfy her. Becky told Beverly that a boy had been talking about fucking and she was embarrassed that she didn't know what he was talking about. Beverly was grateful that she didn't know. That meant that John hadn't hurt her.

Looking back, how could Beverly have known what love was? She had lived with lies, secrets, fear, and pain. She was pretty sure that wasn't love. Or at least what she hoped love was.

Beverly ended up moving back to the city. She had to drink to survive. She doesn't remember having a job. She may have, but it would have been short-lived. Mostly, she sold herself for sex so she could stay in a drunken stupor. The cops would pick her up and her parole officer would leave her in jail for thirty days each time. She could mark off the calendar and then be released. She seldom spoke with her parole officer. Except when she joined Ted and Beverly for a presentation Becky was in at school.

Beverly mainly lived in and out of several subcultures: gay and black. She tried having relationships, but inevitably they would want her to sober up and she would leave. She whored in several late-night houses, but mostly hustled out of bars, turned tricks in sleazy downtown hotels, and vehicles. Most nights she made around a hundred dollars at twenty dollars a pop.

She tried having a pimp once, but when he took a credit card for new tires instead of cash, she decided she could do better, especially when the card was no good.

The pimps left Beverly alone, except one day when she was walking down a brick sidewalk in heels. She was watching where she was walking so she didn't get her heels stuck between the bricks. One pimp stopped his car and said, "You get your head up! You're a fox! Now look like it!" He drove away and never said anything else to her. I suppose that her reputation about flipping out unexpectedly might have kept them from trying to intimidate her. Apparently they didn't know that she had built that reputation on purpose.

Beverly was placed in a rural nursing home by her parole officer. She worked there for a few days before calling a couple that had been in prison with her that lived a couple states away. They told her to come out and she started off in her old car. It had a habit of breaking rotors and stopped in the middle of nowhere. She grabbed her bag of clothes and hitchhiked to Omaha where they had sent her a bus ticket. When she arrived she called her friends, and they picked her up. They all ended up going to another state where one of their parents lived.

That was an interesting trip, their old car with three adults, four or five kids, and no air conditioning in the middle of summer. They even drove through Salt River Canyon where Beverly was sure they were going to die. God takes care of fools and drunks.

Beverly called Ted for money and he wired it to her. All three of them went out to celebrate. Beverly was just getting started drinking good when the other two wanted to go home. She told them she would be there later, but the next morning she came out of a blackout in a car quite a few miles from where her friends moved.

The man driving it said he was some kind of an inspector for the Indians. He said that he was going to inspect a school in the middle of nowhere. Beverly looked around and that's where they were, in the middle of nowhere. She thought, *Great, this is where it will end for me; buried under a rock and no one will ever find me.* The next thought was, *At least it will be over*. She relaxed.

But the man didn't stop the car. They drove past stick huts with new single car garages. The man said that the government had built the buildings for the Indians to use as homes, but they were letting their animals live in them. He showed her a place that he called Fort Apache. It was a foundation filled with weeds. He really was an inspector.

They stopped at a new schoolhouse. He entered the building and left her in the car for a couple of hours. When he returned, he drove her to the interstate highway where she caught a ride with a semi driver.

The truck driver was fun because he had drugs and they stayed awake all the way to Iowa.

Beverly got back to the city and met Phil at a gay bar. She lived with him for a while. He treated her better than anyone had ever treated her, but she knew that she couldn't fight his urge to be with men.

Then she met Greg. What a guy! He taught her what sex was

supposed to be like. The problem was that he also liked to beat the hell out of her. One night she got out of the hotel room and found a ride to Ted's farm. Her face was so black and swollen that Becky screamed when Beverly came down the stairs the next morning. Beverly still healed fast in those days, but not nearly fast enough to not scare Becky. She still feels bad about everything she put her sister through in those years.

A few days later, Ted and Becky were not home. Greg came to the farm. He left real fast when Beverly started shooting at his car with Ted's pump shot gun. She went to bed, but Ted woke her up with fear in his eyes when they got home because she had left the spent shells on the steps to the house. Becky told her later that they were scared that she was dead. It wouldn't have bothered Beverly if she was.

Beverly couldn't take it any longer. She wanted to go back to prison where she was safe. It sounds funny to feel safe in prison, but at least she could sleep at night in her own room, had three meals a day, and clean clothes. She was tired.

Beverly took one of Ted's checks, filled it out, forged his signature, and cashed it in a grocery store. The next time she was picked up for being drunk, disorderly conduct, and having her face bashed in, her parole officer put a hold on her, transferred her to the county jail, and pulled her parole. She went back to prison after two years and one day of drunken madness.

This time she rested in isolation, knew how to use the cigarette roller, and was welcomed back by old acquaintances. What had she learned? She learned that she wouldn't take another parole. She'd watched people leave on parole and come back numerous times. Some of them, like Donna, just gave up and became institutionalized. No! That wasn't going to happen to her! She would do her time and leave free. No matter how long it took.

This time, at different times, she was the drug room girl that sprayed the new prisoners with bug spray and typed reports. She was the store room girl that documented the items women brought in with them and made sure it was all there when they left. She was a farm girl that mowed the grounds with a tractor and helped take care of the pigs.

Oh, do you remember the woman she first met in prison. The one that had helped her husband tie their son to the bed, set the house on fire, and stood outside and listening to him scream while he burned to death? Well, it was a few years later, and Beverly isn't very proud of what she did, but it sure felt good at the time! They were alone while cleaning out the hog house. Somehow the woman slipped in the manure and ended up eating quite a bit of it. She swallowed it too!

One day Beverly was offered the opportunity to make a dollar a cut of fabric to make custom drapes. Let's see. She could make a dime, quarter or thirty five cents a day doing the previous details or four to five dollars a day making drapes. She already knew how to sew and it didn't take a brain surgeon to figure this one out! She learned to make custom drapes. Fiberglass drapes. She had two uniforms to wear while making them because the fiberglass permeated the fabric and itched constantly. Showers didn't remove the glass from her skin and changing into clothing that was not contaminated didn't stop the itching. But she got to go off campus to measure and hang the drapes. She got meals in restaurants. And the biggest benefit was that the sewing room was air conditioned. To this day she refuses to be around fiberglass.

Speaking of air conditioning, only the employee offices, drug room, sewing room, and matron's quarters were air conditioned. Beverly slept many nights on the polished concrete floor with her mouth to the bottom of the door to get air. The inmates weren't even allowed fans in their rooms until the late '60s.

Prisoners couldn't even look at a telephone, let alone use one to call anyone. Beverly doesn't remember any of the prisoners getting to use one when there was a family emergency. Messages were relayed through the employees.

There were inmate cliques. Beverly doesn't remember being an inner part of any of them. She got along with the black women and a few whites. Mostly she kept to herself and did her time.

When Beverly's room was at the top of the stairs, she jiggered (stopped the matron from catching the numerous lovers down the hall) and received a pack of cigarettes from each couple. Needless to say, she didn't have to roll any cigarettes during that period.

Oh, cigarettes were twenty-five cents a pack. Tobacco, papers, and matches were furnished by the facility. Beverly could use the "cottage" roller or buy her own. She bought her own. It was high-tech for the time. It was blue and spit out the final product when she folded it in half to close it. She rolled many a cigarette watching TV in the bay through those years.

Cigarettes seemed to be the only constant in her life. She could count on them to do what they were supposed to do. She still hasn't quit smoking even with COPD. She says that smoking is better than sucking her thumb in public. She'd like to blame the cigarette companies, advertising agencies, and movies that equated smoking with being sophisticated and cool when she was growing up, but that excuse doesn't work anymore. She knows better, but just hasn't found the courage to stop.

Speaking of TV, there was only one in each cottage and the inmates voted what they watched. It got rather interesting once in a while. Cliques would run around trying to get votes prior to the important time, most of the time Beverly went to her room and stayed out of it.

Beverly learned to knit during her incarceration. She made Barbie Doll clothes for Becky's doll. The woman that taught Beverly to knit helped her make cable sweaters and all types of dresses. She learned a few years later that Becky sold the doll and her wardrobe to Teddy's wife. Too bad, it would have been worth a lot of money today and Becky is all about money.

Beverly tried being with a lesbian several times, but she just couldn't get the concept. Women were ill-equipped to finish the job. But then, she did like being held. Skin contact had been missing from her life, without sex or beatings involved, for many years. Masturbation was her choice. It was less problematic.

Beverly was able to have sex a few times with some of the men that worked at the prison. It was fast and usually unfulfilling for her, but it felt good to be held. Besides, she had learned as a child not to expect anything for herself from men.

"Ol' Three Hairs" retired and a man was the temporary warden for a while. Beverly doesn't remember his name, but he offered her the opportunity to become the first woman in Iowa to participate in a new program. It was called work release. She was to attend business college in a neighboring town during the day and return to prison every evening. Again, a rocket scientist she isn't, but this seemed like a good idea to her. She accepted. She rode back and forth with a girl from town.

Beverly doesn't know how she ever completed that semester. She didn't feel comfortable with the other students. They knew where she lived and kept their distance. She drank her lunches at a nearby bar and sometimes didn't get back to class on time. Actually, she should be applauded for returning at all. Usually when she started drinking, she didn't quit until she blacked out. You see, they didn't have AA the second time Beverly was incarcerated. She was told that it was discontinued when the AA men were caught servicing the female inmates while Beverly was on parole.

Beverly shared with the woman that a similar thing happened to her when she first got out on parole, "I don't know who to trust. I really believe that AA works, but if all men want is sex from me, that isn't what the book says they are supposed to do."

One evening on the way back to Rockwell, the radio announcer said that one of our spy planes had been captured by the Russians. Beverly remembered the week of classes she had attended about what to do during nuclear war. It seems that the reformatory's tunnel was to be the haven for everyone in town and the prisoners were to make sure that all were safe.

Beverly's initial reaction to the radio announcement was that she needed to get this car away from the girl and find a bar. The girl seemed to sense what was going on in Beverly's head, but they had become friendly during the days of travel and Beverly just couldn't hurt her. "It's all right." They both relaxed and talked about how their country could be in deep crap.

It turned out all right. The US didn't go to war with Russia, but the Viet Nam veterans returning from fighting for our country were being spit on. Beverly didn't understand why it was their fault. It seemed to her that they had probably lived through enough hell and didn't deserve unkind treatment from the people they were trying to protect. She still believes that!

Somewhere during this time there were two more women added to the work release program and an apartment was set up for all three on the top floor of the industrial building. One of them was all right, but Beverly had threatened the other one with being the bottom of the food chain during their fall-out shelter training. She meant it at the time. Her opinion of the woman hadn't changed and the living arrangement was not one of her favorite experiences.

The business college Beverly had been attending closed. The inmate she got along with started junior college with her. The other prisoner was doing time for second degree murder. Two horny alcoholics should never be put together on the "outside" for hours at a time, especially if they have no access to AA meetings.

They attended classes for a few weeks and felt very out of place. They got some of the basketball stars from New York to rent motel rooms and get beer in the afternoons and enjoyed sex with them.

It occurred to Beverly that she was going to get pulled from the work release program as soon as her school records arrived at the prison because she had skipped so many classes. She contacted several people and had rides set up to a town on the other side of the state, but the other prisoner threatened to "snitch" if she didn't take her. Off they went. Beverly called it a much deserved vacation, but knew it was really escape.

Becky told Beverly years later that she and Ted were eating lunch when the newscaster said something to the effect that two women had escaped from the women's reformatory and gave Beverly's name as one of the escapees. Because the one prisoner was doing time for second degree murder, they were both considered, according to the newscaster, to be armed and dangerous. Becky said that she and Ted just sat there looking at the TV for a long time with their forks in midair.

Becky said that she was sent to stay with her boyfriend's family and Ted stayed home and waited for Beverly's arrival.

Beverly and the other prisoner arrived at their destination after dark. They went to a dingy, black bar. Beverly turned a few tricks and made the money she needed for some clothes, toiletries, and a hotel room in another city. She talked a man into giving her a ride there and said adios to the other woman.

Beverly got a hotel room for a week, some booze, and settled in. The isolation got overwhelming in a couple days and, with enough booze, the fear of being caught subsided. She started drinking at a bar on one of the main avenues where cops hung out. She'd learned a long time ago that the best way to not be found is to be right under their noses. Some of them even bought her beer.

After a week Beverly was tired, not horny any more and sick from drinking that much. She asked a man to drive her to Ted's farm. He dropped her off on the road and she walked into the house, took a bath, and went up stairs to change her clothes. When she came back down, Ted was sitting at the kitchen table. She sat down in her assigned spot. Neither of them said anything for a long time. After all, what could she say?

Finally Ted said, "I'm not going to help you."

Beverly asked, "Are you going to turn me in?"

"Nope."

Her mind raced. She was seven and one half miles from one town and eleven miles from another. All of the surrounding farmers had heard about her escape by now and would gladly turn her in for the reward. Besides, where would she go? Life of the run didn't sound like that much fun. Beverly asked, "Will you take me to the county jail?"

"Yup."

Ted drove in silence, stopped at the jail, Beverly got out, and he drove away. She was getting used to being left alone. She had struggled to keep John away from her and Becky, no one had helped her when Ann was emotionally and physically pummeling her, Ann had left her alone to find a way to retrieve her watch and she learned to turn tricks for money, Ted and her family had left her alone in her apartment after her baby and Ann were killed in the car accident, she had little communication from any of her family while she was incarcerated, and now Ted drove away without even a wave. No wonder she felt isolated and unloved.

Beverly walked to the screen door.

"Can I help you?" a woman's voice came from inside.

"I think you are looking for me. I'm Beverly."

"Oh," she said, "come around to the next door."

Beverly did so, but her mind objected. *Hey, I'm supposed to be armed and dangerous here!* But then she realized that the county authorities knew she was harmless when she wasn't drinking or provoked. After all, she had been a trustee a few years ago while she waited to go back to prison on parole violation.

A couple from prison came after Beverly and she was transported back to its peace and quiet. That scared her because she recognized that she was becoming institutionalized like Donna and others. She was facing five additional years for the escape. She became more determined than ever to do her time and leave free. She knew for sure that she would never be able to complete a parole. She wasn't going to quit drinking and that would violate her parole every time.

Beverly was given five extra months for the escape instead of five years. She was told that it was because she had turned herself in and she did not stay out very long or run.

Beverly doesn't remember what detail she had when she came out of lockup and isolation. She just put her head down and walked through the time. She must have behaved herself because she was offered another chance to participate on work release. Once again she accepted. She worked at a national furniture store chain. She dusted furniture and learned how to sell it.

She enjoyed working there. The man that owned the store turned out to be a distant cousin, but neither of them knew it at the time. His wife didn't act like she liked Beverly much, but she tried to be pleasant. She taught Beverly much about furniture construction, classification and style.

On the way to work one day Beverly saw a beautiful car with about a foot of snow all over it. It was a 1965 red Pontiac convertible with a white top. She wrote Ted that she would like to have it when she got out in a few months. She told him that she had some money from working and would like to borrow the rest from him. The next time he and Becky came to visit, Becky was driving Ted's car and Ted was driving Beverly's Pontiac. He told her that it would be in the machine shed waiting for her when she was released.

During Christmas Beverly was allowed to work and stay in a hotel in the city. The new female warden picked her up. Beverly was in a drunken stupor. She took her to her house, fed her coffee, and told her, "You are going to ruin work release!" She sobered Beverly up and took her back to the apartment. She was pulled from work release again.

Several months before Beverly completed her time, she was taken to the hospital to have her wisdom teeth removed. She was told that she never had the top two, but the bottom ones were growing with their roots around her other teeth. She was knocked out and her bottom wisdom teeth were cut out.

She awoke to the intravenous bottle not dripping. She had been a nurse's aid while she was on parole and knew this was not a good situation. She waved at the people walking down the hall, but they waved back. She waved and pointed at the intravenous bottle, but they waved and smiled. She finally gave up and passed out again.

When she woke up, a nurse and her doctor were working on the bottle. He told her, "Beverly, if you can drink liquids, we will take this out of you."

She said through the packing they had in her mouth, "Give me the fuckers!"

She ran the nurses ragged for water and juices when she was awake, but they kept coming in and asking her if she was in pain. She would nod and they would give her a shot that she REALLY liked. Off she'd go into never-neverland until the scenario was repeated. She doesn't know how many days this went on, but it seemed like a lot. Finally, she asked the nurse, "What are you giving me?

"Morphine."

Beverly almost crawled through the wall behind the headboard, "NO! I CAN'T AFFORD MY BEER! YOU AREN'T GOING TO MAKE ME INTO A DRUG ADDICT, TOO!!!"

Beverly was returned to prison. The idiots sent morphine tablets with her. She told the doctor she didn't need them, but he didn't know or care about the problems the drugs were to cause in her life. The drug room girl let the entire drug addict population in prison know that she had them available to her and they wanted her to go get them. She told them to go steal them, "I'm getting out in five months, free. You'll regret postponing my release in any way!"

Apparently they believed her because she didn't have any more problems. Maybe they did steal them.

Beverly doesn't remember what detail she had those last months. She thinks she returned to the sewing room to make drapes for resale and clothes for her new life on the outside.

Beverly's release date arrived. She had lost weight and made some clothes. Her hair was long and straight. The women in the city had a welcome home party planned for her. She was twenty four and ready to party, but Becky was graduating from high school that night and getting married the next.

CHAPTER 3

Beverly doesn't remember much about the trip home. It must have been uneventful. She remembers that Ted told her that he would have to get the tractor to pull her car through the mud to the driveway. He said that he'd put the Pontiac in the machine shed to make sure no one drove it but her.

Beverly got to touch, for the first time, the most beautiful car she had ever seen. Sit in it. Hear the motor run. Her red with a white top, 1965, Pontiac, Catalina convertible felt like it had been built just for her. She stroked it like a new, proud parent.

The terror of freedom hadn't hit Beverly yet. There was just so much going on. She was focused on Becky's high school graduation and wedding. She wanted to get drunk and have sex, but knew better than leave the farm before Becky's graduation. She would go to a bar and not come back. It was important to her to wait and attend the graduation ceremony. She hadn't been there for Becky any other time. This time she wasn't going to disappoint her.

Beverly told Becky that she wasn't interested in loaning her and Perry her car the next night for their honeymoon. She didn't want the shaving cream all over it and tin cans tied to the bumper that their friends would put on the car they were using. Besides, she had parties to go to. Women she had done time with were throwing a coming home party in the city after the graduation festivities and she planned on going to a bar and dancing with a man for the first time in years after Becky's wedding. She planned on showing up in her beautiful car with her long straight hair flowing in the wind of freedom as she drove down the road. No, she would drive her own car.

The day was gone before Beverly knew it. She was getting dressed to watch Becky walk across the stage and receive her high school diploma. She put on a yellow skirted, narew collared suit and black turtle neck top. She wore black panty hose with black open-toed heels and a black clutch bag. It was a happy occasion so she wore a bright color, but also wanted to look sexy for later that evening.

Beverly was feeling a little melancholy. She didn't have a high school diploma. She had gotten her GED before her class graduated and she went to prison, but she never finished high school. She got pregnant and girls weren't allowed to continue attending public schools then. "Oh yeah?" she said out loud, "I just completed finishing school!" Then she shook her head. "I sure didn't want to learn some of the things I found out in prison! I sure hope I'm not finished!"

Beverly was really proud of Becky. Not only had she lived through a horrible car accident and the grief of losing Ann and the baby; she had taught herself to walk again and finished high school.

Everyone went back to Ted's farm for Becky's reception. Beverly stayed the allotted time. She had told Ted about the homecoming party for her in the city earlier in the day and he gave her the sign when it was all right for her to leave. She said goodbye and told Becky that she was proud of her. Becky reminded her that she was getting married the next evening and needed her to be home by noon. Beverly told her that she would be there, got into her beautiful convertible and drove down the road.

Beverly felt great. She was twenty four and hadn't had a driver's license since she was sixteen when Ted sent it back to the State because she was very irresponsible with his cars.

Okay, she had ripped off the muffler and tail pipe of his work car going over a railroad track too fast, destroyed a tire by running on it low, and hit a tree trying to kill herself when she found out she was pregnant. She totaled that car. Then she stole his next work car, got drunk, and he and Ann found her in a neighboring town. Gee, wonder why he didn't want her to drive.

Why did he believe her now? They both knew that she would be drinking and driving. Maybe there was a good reason he was the beneficiary of her insurance.

Now Beverly had a great car, driver's license, and insurance. On top of that she was slim with long, straight brown hair. Her legs looked good in heels and the short yellow skirt. She had a full tank of gas, money in her pocket, and was headed for a great party. How could it get any better?

As she drove into the first town, she decided that she would stop for a beer. "Yeah, one beer wouldn't hurt me. Besides, I have been good all day so I could be at Becky's graduation."

Beverly parked, walked into the bar, and noticed that the men had all taken notice of her. At the other end of the bar was her daughter's father. He didn't act like he knew her. She realized that she was still mad that he hadn't claimed being her daughter's father, but she didn't realize how mad she was until he came to the booth and introduced himself.

Beverly had learned in prison to only show emotions that she wanted others to see. She politely introduced herself using her married name. Her brain exploded. *How dare you! Our daughter, who you never met, is lying in the cold ground and now you are trying to pick me up again...you married bastard!!*

Beverly didn't know what she was going to do, but she asked him to sit down. Beverly's thoughts went wild. *He still doesn't recognize me. Was he that drunk when we were having sex? That can't be. We rode the school bus together for years when we were kids. Is he that drunk now?*

They talked for a while. Finally Beverly told him that she was heading for a party in the city and he could come along if he wanted to. She told him that they could bar hop all the way there. He told her that he had to be back in time to go to work the next morning because he would be fired if he wasn't.

Beverly internally smiled. *I'm going to get even.*

Smiling suggestively, she said, "Of course I will have you back in time."

They stopped at bars all the way to the middle of the city. By that time it was past midnight and Beverly was ready to go to the party. She stopped at a drugstore where gay people hung out and asked him to go in and get her a hamburger. "I'll drive around the block until you come out."

He agreed and got out of the car.

Beverly went to the party. "Let him explain that to his wife!"

Beverly got up the next morning with a hangover, but not nearly as bad as it used to be. She drove to Ted's farm in time to do the things that Becky needed her to do for the wedding. Becky was still trying to get her to let them use her car for their honeymoon, but Beverly was steadfast and Becky finally gave up.

Becky's wedding was more emotional that Beverly expected. She never understood why people cried at weddings until that night. Watching Becky walk down the isle in her white wedding gown on Ted's arm took Beverly's emotions by surprise. Her brain rushed through all of the good and bad things Becky had lived through. Beverly was so proud of her that she almost burst. Ted presented Becky to the minister and Perry and sat down next to Beverly.

That night, watching Becky marry Perry, Beverly remembered the promise she had made to Ann when she was pregnant with her daughter. Ann had made her promise to take care of Ted if anything happened to Ann. Beverly made the promise, but never expected that she would have to fulfill it. Now here she was. How could she possibly fill her mother's role in the family? Ann was so perfect. After all, hadn't the church been packed for her funeral? Didn't everyone always tell Beverly how lucky she was to have such a wonderful mother?

The blackness of depression settled in on Beverly that night. The guilt of praying that Ann would die so she could have her baby and their deaths along with feeling responsible for Becky's injuries in the car accident was more than she could stand. Every cell in her body screamed for relief.

Beverly took Ann's place as mother of the bride in the wedding pictures, but felt totally unqualified to do so.

The wedding reception was in the basement of the church Beverly had been raised in. She had attended and taught Sunday school in that basement before all hell broke loose in her life. She prayed that Becky's life would be better than hers. She prayed that Becky's marriage would be long and happy.

Ted knew that he wouldn't see Beverly much when she left the church that night. She had some drinking to do. She was horny, thirsty, and wanted to dance her ass off! She had been locked up for years. She was off and running. She felt like a colt that had just been let out of the barn in a spring pasture full of new playmates.

Beverly knew she was an alcoholic, but at that point, she didn't care. She had no perception of how dangerous she was to herself and the public. She fully intended to do whatever she wanted for the foreseeable future. Her first priority was to drink enough beer and dance with enough men to make the depression go away. That is as far into the future as she could see. She'd been waiting for this moment for years. She had dreamed about how it would feel, but her dreams could not measure up to the exhilaration of the moment.

As an ex-con, Beverly had three employment options: waitress, bartender, or whore. She did all three. She drank, used drugs, and drove her car hard back and forth between the farm and the city. Many times, as she drove home in the early mornings, trees beside the highway would move into her lane. Her brain would tell her that they couldn't do that, but there they were. She would slow down and cautiously stay in her lane. As the car moved through the trees, the trees would slide back to their original place. She suspected that she was overdosing, but she didn't care. Oblivion, even death, was preferable to the abyss of depression.

Beverly tried to find a place for herself, but she didn't fit anywhere. She never had. Not even in the bars, certainly not with her family.

Teddy had not spoken to her the whole time she was incarcerated. Becky was married and off in her new life. Ted didn't say much, but she believed he wanted her to do well. She just didn't know how to get there.

People from the criminal justice system were hounding Beverly's family by telephone trying to contact her. They wanted to send her to college. She knew that they were just trying to get her back under their control. They weren't fooling her! She had done her time and it was none of their business what she was doing. She finally had to threaten to sue them to stop the telephone calls.

Of course, today she wishes she had taken advantage of the offer, but knows that she was incapable of seriously investing herself and her energy in an education at that time. She wishes it would have been different.

Beverly doesn't remember how long it was after her release, but it seems like three or four months. The motor in her car was knocking and she had finally given up trying to find a positive life. She knew others could, but she never would.

She was at the gas station in a small town. Becky and Perry were there. She could see that they were happy. God, how Beverly wanted to be happy.

Beverly asked Perry, "Is my insurance paid?"

"Ya?"

Beverly didn't say anything. She just drove west, hard and fast. The next thing she knew, the motor clanked and seized up. She had looked at the speedometer right before all hell broke loose and it said that she was going well over 100 miles per hour. She flipped the steering wheel to the right as hard as she could and relaxed for death.

Somebody told her later that she spun into the opposite ditch, across the highway in front of a truck, and into the other ditch. All she knew was that she slid backwards beside the fence and came to a stop. "Dam it! I can't even kill myself right!!"

Becky was there screaming at her, "Get fucked!"

Beverly told Becky to get out of there and she left.

Ted had Beverly's car towed and a mechanic put in a new short block. Apparently, some of the rods had gone through the pan. He had a 389 put in. Maybe he thought that would slow her down. Meanwhile, he loaned Beverly his second car to drive back and forth to work. He didn't know that she had quit her job as a waitress at a small truck stop near the interstate after a few days. That she used it in the city to go from bar to bar.

John, Beverly's molester, was in a nursing home. Ted asked her if she wanted to go see him. She told him, "I will for you!"

Beverly doesn't know if Ted knew about his father molesting her. If he did, he never gave any sign of it. She is sure he knew that she didn't like John because she was very obvious about her contempt for him. She never tried to hide it.

As they entered the building Ted said, "He may not know you. He's been having shower strokes for a long time."

Mary was sitting in a chair next to John's bed. She and Beverly nodded at each other as she passed. Beverly didn't think anything about Mary not offering her a hug or any other sign of affection. She had never been affectionate. In fact, none of Beverly's family had been affectionate unless you count John's molestation.

John had been a six foot tall muscular German with a pot belly. The man that lay in the bed was a withered, skinny shell of that person. His face was sunk in. He looked like he was asleep. Beverly picked up his hand. "Grandpa?"

His eyes opened and immediately filled with tears.

"Do you know who I am?"

He nodded with a weak, "Beverly," and started sobbing. His eyes begged her to forgive him.

Beverly held his hand for quite a while looking into his imploring eyes. The pain he had caused by molesting her melted away. She was shocked that she could still feel any type of compassion for him, but she did. He was dying. If she didn't forgive him, he might not go to heaven.

Finally she patted his hand, "Its all right Grandpa…It's all right." She dropped her eyes and nodded; laid his hand back on the bed and walked to the car. She had a cigarette while she waited for Ted.

Beverly's brain exploded. *Why didn't I say something? Why didn't I yell and scream at him? Why didn't I make them admit that they have always known that he hurt me? Why couldn't they have been there for me when I needed them most? Why am I still keeping silent? Why didn't I make Dad admit that he hurt me when he pulled Mom off of me and held her instead of my bloody body? What is wrong with me that nobody cares?*

John died several days later. It felt to Beverly like he had hung on until she visited him and said that she forgave him. She's not sure that she ever did. All she knew was that, for whatever reason, she had to play the hand she was dealt. So did he.

Beverly was using Ted's car while her Pontiac was getting the motor rebuilt. She got to her grandparent's home just in time for Ted to clean the garbage and empty beer cans out of his car and drive them to John's funeral.

The minister talked about how wonderful John was. He'd put the roof on the church, helped with repairs, etcetera. Beverly wasn't that impressed and wondered what everybody would do if she went to the front of the church and told the rest of the story. After all, Ann was dead and couldn't kill her. Then she remembered that it would hurt Ted and resisted the impulse.

Beverly's beautiful red convertible had its new motor and she was driving it again. She loved the way the front lifted and the back sat down when she hit the gas. She loved the feeling of power and freedom when she drove down the highway with the top down with the wind blowing in her long straight hair. She was determined that no one would ever lock her up again. After all, the one thing that prison had taught her was to not get caught.

Beverly was looking a little worse for the wear by this time. She mainly went to the black and gay bars. She worked in the night joints, hustled the straight bars, and drank wherever she ended up.

Greg and Beverly hooked up again. He wanted to move to Omaha so off they went. She didn't have anything particular holding her in the city.

Beverly got a nice apartment in one of the western suburbs. Greg stayed with her until she caught him and a woman in each other's arms. She told him something about, "Don't ever talk to me again, if you know what's good for you." He apparently believed her because that was the last she ever heard from him. Of course, he probably remembered her pitting his car with Ted's shotgun. She didn't play games nor did she particularly care about much.

Beverly met Juan in a bar one night while playing pool. He was a Chicano from Chicago and was he ever gorgeous: jet black hair, dark skin with a smile that could melt any woman's heart. He and the bar's owner were friends. Juan and Beverly hooked up and both tended bar at the same place. Beverly took the day shift. She took amphetamines that were prescribed by three doctors. She drank and hustled the bars at night. They lived between Omaha, Chicago, and Iowa. His two oldest nephews came to live with them in Omaha and one of his daughters lived with them for a while in Iowa, but her drinking got worse and they had to take them back to Chicago for their safety.

After Beverly quit hustling and she married Juan, he gave her the clap. He had apparently been having sex with a Native American woman. That woman made the mistake of coming into the bar and asking Beverly, in front of the bar's owner, "Is Juan here?"

Beverly said that he wasn't.

She pointed to Beverly's car. "His car is here!"

The bar owner got real nervous when Beverly told her the time that Juan would be at work. She never came back, but Beverly never got over it. She tried to run over Juan, had a pistol in his face when she came out of a blackout once, shot in his direction several times, and turned the car on when he was putting in the distributor wire they removed so no one would steal the car. He cussed at her. He always cussed her out in Spanish so she didn't know what he was saying. Beverly thought, *That was probably a good idea.*

One night Beverly tried to call Ted. The operator told her that the telephone had been disconnected. Beverly called her everything but a child of God, "My father pays his bills!" and slammed the phone on its cradle.

A few days later, Beverly received a letter from Ted. He told her that he had flushed the stool and that there had been an explosion. Beverly started screaming and crying.

Juan grabbed her by the shoulders and asked, "What the hell is the matter?"

"Dad is dead!"

"He can't be! He wrote the letter!"

The gas had escaped from the underground rock formations below Ted's farm and followed the field tile into his cellar. When he flushed the stool, the water pump sparked igniting the gas, the porches were blown off the house, the kitchen wall was blown out, and the windows shattered. Ted had stood in the bathroom doorway to make sure the water pump kicked in and was saved from the force of the explosion.

Ted bought two houses outside a rural town about eleven miles from the farm. He lived in one and Becky and Perry lived in the other one. He told Beverly that there was a bedroom there for her and bought a bedroom set for it.

The night Beverly left Juan for the last time, she broke a beer glass on the bar and went after him. He was faster than she was. She finally decided that it was best that she use it on herself, but he stopped her and called her crazy. She was. She was certifiably insane at that moment. Her brain exploded. *Why can't anybody love me? Why are they always making me believe them and then showing me that they have lied to me? He said he'd be my husband and then he gave me the clap he got from another woman! What's the use? Why keep trying?*

Beverly went to their apartment and broke everything that would shatter. She grabbed her clothes and belongings and drove out of Omaha at over 100 mph. through red lights. The only reason she can figure that she didn't hit anybody was that it was between 4:00 and 5:00 a.m. God, was she dangerous.

The next one and one half years Beverly lived in Ted's extra bedroom. She spent most of her time drinking in bars. She wrote a note to Ted right after she moved in, *Dear Dad, Am at the bar. Bring money. Love Beverly.*

Ted would turn it face down on the counter, come to the bar, drink with her and give her money. The next day she would turn the note face up on the counter and the sequence repeated itself. One day at a time.

Joe babysat with Beverly for those years. He was her lover, friend and confidant. He was a lot older than she was and married, but his family lived across the state. He told Beverly years later that he poured most of his beer in her mug so he could stay half-way sober and keep her out of trouble. It didn't always work. The owner of the bar either threw her out or threatened to throw her out many times a week.

Beverly didn't work that much during that time. She couldn't keep from drinking. She would try, but she would start shaking and leave work. After a few days of that, she just didn't go back. Finally, she was hired to manage a drapery shop. She hired a woman who had been trained in prison with her to make drapes. But when they were both paid with checks that bounced, they both quit.

Beverly finally got herself together enough to tend bar at the bowling alley. Her job included food distribution. It was no big deal since she had done the same job in Omaha with lots more patrons.

Finally, she borrowed $500 from Ted to buy a sewing machine. He built her drapery tables in his basement and she started Beverly's Drapery.

Beverly doesn't know if Ted really thought she could do it, but the last night she worked at the bowling alley the owner told Ted to talk her out of quitting because he would have to hire two people to do her job. Ted took a drink of his beer and looked at him. "At least she has guts to try!" Beverly smiled at him and finished cleaning up. They left the building and she never looked back.

Beverly started making drapes for a nursing home. The woman that taught her to make drapes in prison contracted one wing to her. She met her instructor at the nursing home to measure the windows and then she drove to the prison to pick up the fabric. While she was there, she spoke with the warden. It gave Beverly great pleasure to see her in that capacity instead of the prisoner she expected Beverly to be again.

Beverly didn't realize it at the time, but the warden had been her first real mentor. She had made Beverly believe that somehow she would be a worthwhile person some day. Beverly wishes that she could tell her thank you now.

After Beverly hung the drapes for the nursing home, she advertised in the county roundup every week. People who originally wouldn't speak to her began to spend thousands of dollars for her to make their window treatments. Each job sold one or two more. Their friends from all over the state called her and she worked hard.

The ten years that Beverly operated her custom drapery and decorating service were crucial in helping her socialize herself and stay out of prison. Her hangovers were always horrendous because whenever she started to drink, she wouldn't quit until she passed out.

Beverly divorced Juan after she met Tom and moved in with him. She moved her workroom to the basement of the Quonset hut where they lived and only drank periodically. Sometimes they would go three months without drinking. When they did, Tom would make sure to vacuum the bedroom so her hangover exploded in her brain. They bowled league with Ted, fished, and she started to believe that maybe she could became half-way normal.

Beverly applied for her restoration of citizenship from the governor during those years and received the document in 1974. She was the first woman to complete her sentence in Iowa that didn't receive this certification when they were released.

She was told before she was released from prison that she had to wait a year before she could apply for it. Since she cared about very little in 1969, other than getting as drunk as she could, she didn't bother to apply for five years. As she recalls, the only reason she asked for it at all was because she wanted to vote.

Beverly was called to the hospital in the city by her family. Mary had a stroke and was dying. Beverly took her turn going in to see Mary. She held Mary's hand and dutifully told her that she loved her. When Mary motioned that she wanted a hug, all of the things Ann, Ted, and Kim told her that Mary had said about her flashed through her brain. She patted Mary's hand, laid it on the bed and walked out of the room. Mary died the next day.

Tom and Beverly attended Mary's funeral. Beverly doesn't remember feeling badly, but funerals always reminded her of her daughter's funeral and she always ended up crying.

Beverly remembered Mary crying a couple years prior to her death because her son died when he was a child. It had been over fifty years for her, but she still couldn't talk about it without crying. Beverly wondered how long those feelings of "what might have been" would haunt her. They were always there when she allowed herself to think about her beautiful daughter dying so young. She found out that she just got used to the feelings, but they never go away.

Somewhere in here Beverly got drunk and blacked out when Tom and she bowled league one night. She came out of the blackout in Omaha the next morning. She called Becky, who lived there, to come get her, but Becky told her no and hung up. She called Tom and walked for hours to get to their meeting place.

On the way home he asked her if she wanted a divorce. What came out of her mouth was, "I wanna go to AA!"

The statement shocked her. She hadn't even thought about AA for years. She knows today that all of the praying she had been doing that day ended with her prayers being answered.

Tom and Beverly went to that first AA group she had attended so many years before when she was on parole. The judge had died by that time, but the men and women still dressed nice. But this time she could dress nice too so she didn't feel so out of place. She had also made a lot of drapes for people who were well-to-do by that time and was more comfortable being around them. She made up her mind that she was going to stay in the program this time.

Beverly did the best she knew how. She went to one meeting a week, talked to her male sponsor every day, read the Big Book, made custom window treatments, and stayed dry for seven months.

Beverly doesn't remember what she was irritated about, probably something small, but she decided that she needed to go bowling in the afternoon. She got to the bowling alley and there was league so she opted to go to the bar to play pool. The next thing she knew it's the next morning and she's calling her sponsor to take her to treatment. He and his wife went to the motel and took her to treatment in the city.

She had just been shown to her room, sat down to contemplate her situation when Tom walked in and told her that he was taking her home.

Beverly didn't drink again for five and half years, but her sponsor had Tom take her to the doctor for "something to take off the edge." The doctor gave her Valium. Yup! That did the trick. If you take Valium like she took it, you wouldn't have any edges either.

Beverly bought five yards of different fabrics for one dollar a yard. She could get a skirt, top, slacks, and jacket out of each piece. She started building a work appropriate wardrobe that she could be proud to wear on her drapery appointments, but Tom's response was, "Mom never had new clothes and you don't need them either."

Shock and bewilderment changed to disgust and determination to be the best person Beverly could be. She ignored his constant disapproval of her having nice clothes and continued to add to her wardrobe. She was using the money she made in her business, was paying at least her share of the bills, and not taking anything away from the family unit.

She had lost over one hundred pounds and felt pretty good about herself until a mechanic "hit on her." He scared her so bad that she went home, started eating and put the weight back on.

Was it the mechanic's attention that scared her or was it her own feelings? He was a stranger. How could he scare her? No, it was that she didn't know how to deal with men hitting on her and she was safe when she was fat. They ignored her when she was fat. Safety was preferable to fear.

Somewhere along the way Beverly put in a bid to do the drapes for the county home and got the job. It was over ten thousand dollars of drapes. She needed more room than the basement of the Quonset house could provide. Beverly called Ted and asked if she could buy the house next to him that Becky's in-laws were living in. He told her that he would have to ask Becky if it was all right with her. Apparently, she gave her permission because Beverly and Tom moved in.

Beverly made the drapes for the county home and bought an above-ground swimming pool with part of the money. Tom put up a fence around the back yard and made a concrete patio.

Ted's house was a mirror image of Beverly's with a two car garage in the middle. She chopped out the over-grown bushes in front of her house and marked off the front steps and sidewalk with stakes and string. Ted and Tom did the concrete work for her steps and sidewalk one weekend and Ted's the next. She borrowed money from the bank. Ted and Tom remodeled the ground floor of her house. They knocking out the walls between the kitchen, living room, and porch. They added a kitchen patio door and living room fireplace. They made the two bedrooms into one large bedroom

Beverly remembers when she told Tom about the remodeling. He said, "Mom never had a new refrigerator and you don't need one either!"

Beverly's response was, "I'm not only talking about a new refrigerator, but all new appliances, cabinets, and a fireplace. If you don't want to be a part of it, then get out of the way. I make enough money to do it by myself."

Beverly's family wasn't used to her not drinking. She invited Becky and her family to swim, but told them that they couldn't bring beer. The next thing she knew, Perry and Ted were walking into the backyard with beers in their hands. She told them that they would have to leave if they couldn't leave the beer alone. They left in a huff and there was considerable distancing between them for a while.

That was difficult because Ted lived next door and Beverly provided a hot meal every evening. She is sure he felt like he was in the middle. All the rest of the family still drank. He drank every evening. But Beverly is sure that he was relieved that she had stopped drinking and getting into trouble. They simply reverted back to the "family way" of dealing with difficult things. They didn't talk about it.

Beverly's family didn't seem to understand. There were times that she would have killed for a beer, but as long as it wasn't in the house or yard, God had time to help her find other ways to deal with whatever was bothering her. She made it a rule that no one brought alcohol into her home. If she was at their home while they were drinking and it bothered her, she could leave. She didn't feel obligated to leave her own home for the same reason. She doesn't know if they ever understood, but they didn't bring booze into her home after that, as far as she knew. Drugs are another matter. God only knows how many drugs they brought and used in her home.

Beverly helped start AA meetings in five farm communities over then next few years. She made drapes and built a good reputation. She read self-help books. Her weight rose and fell with the amount of effort she put into losing it. Tom had a new Dodge van and she had a new Dodge hardtop. He had a painting business that flourished when he could tear himself away from her long enough to finish the jobs. She had a drapery business that kept her very busy and she made good money. She taught Becky how to make drapes and paid her to hem many of them. She made Ted's drapes for his entire house and sold Teddy's wife drapes at low cost.

Beverly helped Ted can and freeze vegetables from his half acre garden in the summer. She made lots of bread and butter pickles that he liked so much. She made sure that there was dinner every evening for all three of them. She was the hostess for many family holiday celebrations. She and Tom were living the life that she had not even dared to hope for.

Beverly listened to self-help tapes that told her that she could have a better life, but she would have to be accountable for her behavior. She parroted the things that made sense to her at AA meetings and tried to understand those that didn't.

Beverly's neighbor visited one afternoon. She told Beverly that she was having an affair. Beverly just looked at her. The woman finally said, "Well, say something."

"What am I supposed to say?" Beverly was in shock.

"You could tell me that you are happy for me."

"I don't think so…I think you're being incredibly selfish. You have a great husband and two wonderful kids. What are you thinking?"

"Yeah, but this guy is rich and really good looking."

"Okay, why don't you tell your husband so he can have the same option?"

"He'd throw me out!"

"Maybe that's what you need!"

The neighbor was silent and left in a huff.

Beverly told Tom what the neighbor had said and they decided that they would not tell her husband because it was none of their business. They both felt bad that their relationship with the neighbors cooled until the only time they spoke was when they were in the garden or yard. Beverly missed that relationship, but wanted nothing to do with the deception.

By this time Beverly was taking Valium to wake up, to go to bed, to keep appointments, to stay in the basement and work, and both going to and coming from the bathroom. She must have been a zombie. Anyway, one night she was working on the yellow shirt she came to call her Valium shirt because she embroidered antique cars all over it while she was taking the medication.

As usual, the TV was on, Beverly was in her recliner and Tom was asleep on the couch. There was a man in convulsions on the screen. The announcer was saying that the man had come off of Valium too fast and that is the reason he was in convulsions. For the first time in a long time Beverly's mind cleared, "What are they talking about?"

The next morning she called the county mental health facility and made an appointment with the psychiatrist. She got right in when she told them what she wanted to discuss. The doctor agreed to allow her to take herself off of the drug slowly. She told him that she would start with two tablets a day; take one half in the morning, at noon, at dinner time, and bed time. The next week she was to take three halves per day and subtract one half tablet per week until she was free of the medication.

That's what she did. To her surprise, she found that she was not nearly as nervous all the time without the medication.

Beverly lost over one hundred pounds through hypnotism. She bought a new wardrobe, made lots of coordinated suits and started feeling good about herself. She attended AA meetings almost every evening and found that she could grasp concepts that had eluded her when she was taking Valium. She finally felt that she was living the life that she wanted.

The neighbor found out about his wife's affair and that she had been using their son to cover her activities with the other man. Their son had been going through hell because she told him that if his father found out about the affair it would be his fault. The poor kid was traumatized. The woman moved to the city with their daughter. The father and son stayed living next door to Beverly.

The neighbor boy came to Beverly's home after school and helped her with chores. Christmas was coming soon and he wanted to buy his father a present. She had an electric mattress pad on their bed and he wanted to get his father one because it would help his arthritis. Beverly told the boy that they could order it and he could pay for it by helping her. They agreed and ordered it by phone that day, but it was back-ordered and wasn't going to get there until after Christmas.

Shortly after Christmas the neighbor asked if his son could stay over night with Beverly and Tom because he was going to a company Christmas party and didn't want to drive home after drinking. They were happy to have the boy stay. Beverly put him to bed that night on the couch and kissed his forehead. She said goodnight and went to bed. Tom got him up the next morning and the boy went home so he could go to work with his father. Tom went to work.

Beverly got up and went to work in the basement later that morning. Within a few minutes the neighbor north of her called and asked what was happening by the river behind Beverly's house. Beverly asked what she meant and the neighbor told her that there were a lot of police cars and an ambulance west of her house. Beverly called the sheriff's office, told them who she was, and asked if prisoners had escaped. She was assured they had not so she went back to work.

A few minutes later the doorbell rang. Beverly went upstairs to answer it. It was the neighbor boy's aunt. She told Beverly that he had been shot. Beverly felt like she had been punched in the gut with a sledge hammer. "How bad?"

"He's gone," she said in monotone. "Will you meet his father in his driveway to tell him? I just can't. He's on his way home."

Beverly didn't know what to say, but instinctively nodded her head and they left. Beverly grabbed her purse and car keys and walked to the garage. She heard someone screaming, "NO! NO! NO!" and realized it was her.

Beverly drove next door, and waited. Her neighbor must have known by the way she looked because he started crying. She knew that there was nothing she could say to help him. She'd been through it when her daughter and Ann were killed. In fact, she doesn't remember much about what was said for the next few days. She went with him to the funeral home while he picked out the casket and made funeral arrangements. She convinced a cosmology friend to do the boy's hair, but had to have her drink a diet Pepsi when they got back to the car because the woman started into shock.

Beverly was civil to the boy's mother, but wanted absolutely nothing to do with her.

Beverly will never know for sure what happened. She knows that the boy was distraught about him being forced to keep his mother's secret from his father. Then he felt like it was his fault when his father found out about the affair. Why he took a pistol to supposedly hunt squirrels that morning has always made her wonder if hunting was his real motive.

The funeral was over, but Beverly's emotional whiplash didn't subside. The boy died the latter part of December. Her daughter had died in the middle of December. Christmas and New Year's were a horrible time of the year for her after that.

Beverly felt guilty about the boy dying because he was the first child that she had tried to get close to since her daughter died. Now he was dead too. Maybe she couldn't care about a child without them dying.

Beverly started slipping into the abyss she had to climb out of after her daughter died. Every time she tried to talk to Tom about it, he told her, "It's over. Forget it!"

Beverly couldn't forget it. She didn't want to drink, but she wanted a bottle of Valium. She did neither, she simply white-knuckled it. The emotional pain was horrible and she had no way to make it quit. She tried praying, but felt no connection. She felt herself emotionally on the edge about to drop off into a place that she would never return from.

She realized that she had never dealt with her daughter's death or the guilt about praying that Ann would die so she could have her daughter. The boy's dying brought everything to the surface.

Beverly had always tried to listen to Tom because he was eleven years older and she thought he was more intelligent, more mature and knew how to handle things better than she did. Now she realized that he was simply trying to duplicate how his father had treated his mother. His mother had been put in a State mental hospital every time she tried to exhibit any type of independence. Hadn't Tom told her that his mother never had new clothes or refrigerator?

"He's not going to treat me that way! I wouldn't have it! My mother tried to control me that way. It didn't work for her either."

Tom started hovering. It got so bad that he couldn't work because he was constantly coming home to see what Beverly was doing. He didn't want her talking to anyone that wasn't in the AA program, her clients or his elderly aunts and uncle. She realized that he was old and she wasn't ready to be old. She was only 39.

He ended up stalking her when she and Becky took a break from working in the basement to visit a woman in town for coffee. It got to the point that he didn't want her to invite her family for meals.

The final straw was when he started telling Beverly what she could and couldn't say at AA meetings. "You start keeping our business to us! Chris is dead! Forget it!"

Beverly started attending Alanon meetings so she could talk about the things that were bothering her. She went to AA meetings by herself for the same reason. As her mind cleared from the Valium, she found that she didn't like the way that he treated her. She told him, but he didn't seem able to help himself.

Finally Beverly started spotting and it continued for well over a month. She went to the doctor and he told her, "I don't think its cancer, but we won't close the barn door."

Beverly went to the car and finally broke down and sobbed. She doesn't know how long it was until she could get her grip, but all of the pain flooded out with that river of tears. She felt weak. Then she got mad, "I don't know if I have thirty days or thirty years, but I'm not going to live this way anymore!"

Beverly went home and told Tom that she wanted a divorce and that he needed to move. Tom screamed at her. Ted screamed at her. She was done trying to be the person they wanted her to be. She had feelings and she was going to deal with them whether they liked it or not.

Beverly called the county mental health facility and started counseling. Tom moved next door and stalked her. The neighbor told her later that Tom drove himself crazy not sleeping because he watched the house constantly and drove past it when she returned home from errands and AA meetings or had company.

Beverly made drapes, went to counseling and AA meetings, but wasn't honest about what she was going through. The AA community turned against her because she had thrown Tom out. They didn't know what he was like behind closed doors and it wasn't her place to tell them. Her best friend's husband moved in with her and back with his family. Beverly's life was falling apart and she couldn't find anything to hang on to.

It finally happened. It had been five and one half years since Beverly had tasted alcohol. She was in the gas station after filling up her car. She walked to the beer cooler and bought a six pack of light beer. She remembers thinking something about not ever tasting light beer. All she really remembers is that she popped the top of one of the cans before she started the car. She drove out of town and back. All six cans were gone.

Beverly went to the bar where she usually met Ted to have a soda, but this time she ordered another light beer in front of him. He sat back. "WHAT?!"

She confronted him with, "I'll talk to you tomorrow! You know better!"

He left and she sat alone with her beer. She drank it and ordered another. This went on for quite a while. The next thing she remembers is being in the back room of the restaurant where the members of AA go after the Tuesday meeting. She vaguely remembers being there, or maybe she has been told so many times that she was that she has made up the memories.

AA members told her through the years that she said something about where they could put AA. Today she knows that she was trying to ask for help the only way she knew how.

The next thing she remembers is waking up in her bed. It was morning and a male AA member was yelling at her. He was telling her that she should be a stripper because she was so good at it. It seems that he had driven her home in her car after the bar closed so she didn't get into an accident, kept her keys and walked back to town for his car. He threw Beverly's keys at her and walked out.

Beverly made it to the restroom and back to bed. The hangover was one of the worst she'd ever had. The phone rang and the owner of the bar where she had been drinking the night before asked her to not work on her drapes. Beverly assured her that she would not be working on any drapes that day and hung up.

Later she got up and went to the basement. She was hoping that someone had called to see if she was all right, but no one had. She was standing in front of the answering machine feeling sorry for herself because she had been there for so many others through the years, but when she needed help there wasn't anybody willing to help her.

Ted came down the steps and put his arm around Beverly's shoulders. "Had enough?"

"Oh, God yes! Once every five and a half years is enough for me!"

He hugged her and they went upstairs, but she would live to regret that statement. When she was sober again for five and a half years, she had a heck of a time not drinking. Somehow she believed that she should be able to drink every five and half years. She didn't, but she sure wanted to for over a year.

Beverly put herself in out-patient substance treatment in the city. She made drapes during the day and went to treatment in the evenings. She asked Tom if he would like to be her concerned person. He agreed as long as he could ride to and from treatment with her. She found out that his motive for doing so was to try to make her feel guilty about wanting to divorce him. He wasn't interested in helping either of them stay sober. He used every dirty trick he could think of while they were traveling. Finally, after several days, she called him and told him that he was welcome to continue attending treatment with her because the treatment was free for him, but he would have to drive separately. He refused. He went back to drinking and stalked her until she remarried. Then he moved to the neighboring town, drank himself into a coma blaming her and died.

Beverly continued treatment, received grief counseling, and attended aftercare by herself. She was able to be honest in her sharing and learned a lot of tools to help her stay sober. She divorced Tom.

Beverly still didn't understand all of the concepts of self-actualization. They say that it isn't old behavior when you continue doing it. Anyway, she met Homer during treatment. He was divorced, had a good job working on x-ray equipment in one of the hospitals, had retired from the Navy, and seemed to understand the AA program.

They said in treatment to not get involved for one year so Beverly and Homer got married. What a fiasco that was! He never sobered up for any length of time. She worked as an alcohol and drug counselor. She and his brother ended up committing him to the mental ward at the county hospital.

Homer told Beverly that he didn't want to be married to an ex-con because his security clearance was jeopardized. "After all, I was a sailor on submarines and a company commander."

Beverly didn't know what all of that had to do with already being married to her, but she applied to the governor for a pardon. She submitted all of the required documentation and pretty much ended up forgetting about it until the day they were packing the house to move out of state because Homer had gotten a different job.

The governor's office called and asked if Beverly could meet with the governor. She told them that she was packing and leaving the state. She thanked the person and said that she would just forget the whole thing. A few minutes later the same person called back and asked if she could come to the capital the next morning. She said that she could.

Beverly didn't know what to expect as she drove to the city. Her parole officer had told her to just forget it because the governor didn't give pardons. She figured that he would just laugh in her face and send her away, but he didn't. He talked to her for a while and she told him that she was mad at him because, according to the newspaper, he had fired one of his employees for being an alcoholic. He told her that she didn't know all of the circumstances. She accepted that answer because he seemed to be genuine.

He said, "I read your record. You must have been something else!"

"I was."

"What happened?"

Beverly told him that she joined AA, made window treatments for all types of people, and took pride in her work. She told him that she used self-help books and tapes to help her understand how to live a better life because, "They certainly didn't teach me that in prison."

Finally, he signed her pardon and they both had tears in their eyes.

Beverly hadn't realized until that moment how much it meant to her for someone to believe in her, especially a governor. She had no idea how important that document was or how many doors of opportunity would open because of it. She promised him that she would try to not let him down and left his office.

When Beverly got home she handed the pardon to Ted. She was crying by that time. It was important to her that he read it because he had been about the only person to stick with her most of the time during the bad days of her alcoholism. Sometimes even he wasn't that happy to see her. The rest of the family were usually only around when they wanted something from her.

Beverly and Homer moved to a Gulf state. He disabled his car shortly after they arrived and left it that way. He used her car to go to work and was gone for days on end.

Beverly called Ted and Homer's brother to come retrieve her. Homer moved back to Iowa with her and then took another job in another southern state. He promised that everything would be different there. He not only continued drinking, but became abusive. He never hit her, but she figures he remembered what she told him in the beginning, "Don't ever hit me and plan on sleeping again. I will melt a can of Crisco and pour it all over you!"

Beverly pulled a lot of U-Haul trailers back and forth to Iowa in the next three years. She'd leave Homer, he'd promise to change and she'd go back. She tried so hard because she didn't want to fail in another marriage.

Finally they moved across the state to a small community where he got another job fixing X-ray equipment. They rented a duplex and she hoped it would be different. It was. It was worse. He threw a glass of iced tea all over her white dress when she asked him to accompany her to an AA meeting and dance. She left without a word.

Her sponsor took her home with her that night. The next morning she went to the duplex to once more pack her things and leave, but Homer had changed the locks. Homer had apparently rented the apartment in his name only and the police wouldn't let her break in to retrieve them. This time she left for the last time.

Beverly remembered that she was supposed to pray for the people that she resented. She had prayed for Kim for many years before she accepted that she was a very sick person. Beverly had prayed for Kim to have all the good things that Beverly wanted for herself. She heard that Kim had married a millionaire.

Now it was time for her to pray for Homer so she could get rid of the resentment she felt toward him. She prayed that God would give him all the happiness and good things that she wanted for herself. She had to pray many times on that trip to really mean it, but by the time she got to Kansas she knew in her heart that he was a sick man the needed all of God's grace. She also knew that she hadn't been brought this far to be dropped on her head. She was going to be all right. She was going to stay sober. What a gift!

Emotions affect the body. While Beverly was married to Homer, she had an upper GI and Ted had a lower GI, but nothing was found to be physically wrong with either of them. After she returned home, all of their symptoms disappeared. Beverly was broke, but she was sober. She and Ted were both healthy. What a blessing.

It was Christmas again. Beverly literally had no money. What she learned during that holiday season was that there were people who truly cared about her. She didn't have to buy their love. They gave her presents and she had nothing to give in return. That was probably the first time she knew what humility felt like. She had always thought it meant humiliation. It didn't. She was shown what God's grace is. It was all right to just be herself. She will always be grateful for that experience.

Homer showed up at the AA social club in the city a few weeks later. He told Beverly that he had brought some of her belongings. He had left them at his brother's home. He asked her to come back. "We had such a good thing!"

Beverly was shocked. "We apparently have different opinions of what a good thing is. There is no way I want anything to do with you."

He left and they were divorced.

CHAPTER 4

Beverly couldn't hear the tires on the road so she knew that she was driving on ice, but the truck hadn't broke traction so she drove on.

The moon was full. For a change there wasn't any wind. The mountain looked like glistening waves that had been frozen in time.

Country Western was mellow; cranked up so that Beverly could feel the base. Her thoughts wandered to other women who must be cuddled up in the arms of their man safe and warm. "What's the matter with me?" she said out loud. "Why can't I find someone to love me? I'm not ugly or real stupid. I'd like to have an Ozzie and Harriet life, too!"

Just then she had one of her moments of clarity. "Harriet didn't drive a Peterbuilt! I'm not going to have that kind of relationship."

Something else occurred to Beverly, she hadn't seen any traffic coming from the other direction. "Oh sure, wait 'til we're on top and close the road. That's all right; we're used to being out here by ourselves, aren't we?"

Beverly shook off the *poor me* mood and lifted her right foot to allow Duke to slow by himself. She always named her truck so she didn't feel so alone and stupid when she talked to it. This one was an extended nose, plum-colored *Pete* with a 425 Caterpillar Engine with lots of lights and chrome.

As she guided the right tires on to the shoulder, she could feel the increased traction as they dug through the thin layer of ice into the gravel. She started down-shifting, "Okay, big boy," she said as she leaned forward a little; all of her orifices tightening, "easy does it now."

Trying to hold 80,000 pounds that bends in the middle from sliding off of an icy mountain had always made Beverly a little nervous. She'd watched other drivers roll off of steep down-grades and tell her over the CB, "Come on, chickenshit!" Most of them had made it to the bottom, but the ones that didn't had taught her that it only takes one second, one mistake to change your life forever...if you still have a life to change.

"Good job, big boy, now let's go home." The ice had only been on top of the mountain. Now the road was clear, the moon was full, and Beverly could relax a little bit. She always felt good driving east out of Cheyenne because she knew that she'd be home in a few hours.

What was home to her now? How did an empty trailer on the outskirts of the city become home? She'd driven truck to pay for it. She didn't have a lot of money while she was paying the lot rent on top of the trailer payments, but it sure felt good to only have $190 lot rent going out now. Besides, the park manager and the neighbors kept an eye on it for her.

Beverly's mind started wandering again. She'd put one husband through truck driving school only to find out that they weren't compatible in the truck. Come to think about it, she'd been married to three of her partners; all of them living separate lives now.

Men were supposed to be supreme in trucks. Her place was to simply take up the slack when he was tired. Even the truck driving school graduate had gotten on her truck and seemed to automatically adopt the attitude, "Me man, you woman, therefore stupid!"

"Excuse me?" She'd been getting trucks back and forth for a few years by herself. He even wanted to use the cruise on ice because he said it would hold steady.

Beverly had quietly asked him, "Please don't do that with me in the truck."

He had looked at her with disgust and put the cruise on. The tractor went left, the trailer went right, she braced herself, and he turned it off. "Okay, so you were right about that one!"

She started breathing again, climbed into the bunk, closed the curtain, shook her head, and drifted off to sleep. If she was going to die, she didn't want to see it coming.

Beverly kept trying to share what had worked for her. Like the time she told him not to back the trailer up over the curb. He backed it up and looked at her with self-satisfaction "Why?"

"Because you don't have any mud flaps on the trailer now."

Another husband that had supposedly been driving truck for years tore off the right mirror on their first trip out together. "Stop!" she had yelled.

He stopped, put the truck right back into reverse, and ripped the mirror off on the rider's door. "Damn it! Why didn't you tell me I was that close?" he had screamed at her.

"I don't have a brake on this side." She got into the bunk and closed the curtain.

That partnership/marriage didn't last long. He couldn't read so she ended up driving her shift, staying up to read the road signs for him during his shift, then it was her turn to drive again. His incessant rage got to be too much one night in Nebraska.

Beverly was driving and he was riding in the jump seat. They were east-bound on I-80 in western Nebraska. It was a dark night, the ones that the moon and stars don't help light up the road? She knew that she was out-running her headlights, but they didn't have any time to spare. She was hammer-down.

She moved out into the left lane so that she could pass two 4-wheelers and an RV. The 4-wheeler that had been tail-gating her for quite awhile moved right along with her. Just as she got beside the RV, she saw a full alligator (truck tire tread) directly in front of her left steering tire. Her husband yelled, "You stupid bitch!"

Beverly tightened her grip on the steering wheel and held it steady, lifted her right foot, and felt the rubber impact the bottom of the tractor. She flipped on her right turn signal and held firm in her lane until the

RV and all three 4-wheelers had passed in the right lane. She eased over to the right shoulder, rolled to a stop, and set the brakes.

Beverly was aware of the continuous profanity being spat at her from the jump seat, but didn't have time to worry about him until she made sure the truck was all right. She put on the flashers and grabbed the flashlight from behind the seat on her way out the door. The weld on the step had been broken and she hit the ground hard.

Beverly turned on the flashlight and got under the truck. She wanted to make sure that the cross-over between the fuel tanks hadn't been damaged. It wasn't. She checked for air leaks and there weren't any. In fact, the only damage she could find, other than some dirt missing, was the broken step.

The whole time her husband was standing by the front of the truck. He babbled about her lack of intelligence, the inbreeding of her ancestry, and she is sure that she had ignored some of the really good stuff. She stood up and screamed, "Get in the fucking truck!"

They were both silent as they climbed into the truck. Beverly put it in gear and went through all fifteen gears as her mind accelerated too. This made the second time they had tried to drive together. He'd wanted to get off of the truck a few months before. She had kept her marriage vows and stayed with him. She had contacted the State vocational rehabilitation agency to test him so that maybe he could learn to read and be more independent. She was tired of reading the whole menu to him every time they went to a restaurant.

His counselor helped her get him enrolled in community college learning upholstery. Just like the three times she had found him help to learn to read, he found reasons that he couldn't do it. "Why don't you call the trucking company and see if we can go back out on the road?" he had pleaded.

Beverly shook her head and looked at him for awhile. Then, "Okay," she had told him, "but this time if I quit anything, it's going to be the marriage and not the driving. You start yelling and cussing at me this time and you'll find yourself divorced!"

Beverly doesn't know how many miles she had driven. Her mind continued through the pros and cons of this marriage. Finally she said in a monotone voice, “Of course, you realize that you’re divorced.”

“Well, you scared me!” he whined.

“I was scared, too, but I did a good job! Nobody got hurt and the truck is reparable. A hug, maybe even an atta-boy-girl is what I needed. Apparently you’re incapable of those things.”

Nothing more was said on the way home. Beverly called the safety department when they stopped for fuel. She told them that she refused to go back out on a truck with her husband and that they would be getting a divorce as soon as possible. The company ran them with other partners for awhile until they realized that she was serious.

Beverly drove with her new partner, Sandy, until Sandy bought her own tractor. Beverly’s husband went a few turns with another man. Beverly is not sure what happened between him and his new partner because she never asked anyone. All she knows is that he was drinking a lot and she had to have the telephone and all of the utilities turned off to get him to move out of her mobile home after the divorce. She heard that he ended up losing his license again after hitting the rear end of a semi while he was drunk. She also heard through mutual friends that he’d moved back to his parent’s home.

Beverly said out loud, “Maybe that’s it. Maybe I just won’t accept my role as a woman. Maybe other women are willing to be yelled and cussed at like a dog, but I’m not! It must have something to do with it because the trucking school graduate’s constant bitching and nagging was the reason that I got off of the truck and divorced him, too.”

It was a few days before Christmas. The dispatcher had told Beverly that they could be home for Christmas if they’d take a load to Shaky (Los Angeles). He’d promised that there would be a load back to the city waiting there for them. Of course, after they delivered the load their return load had already been given to another team.

The trucking school graduate raged. He acted as if she had lied to him about being home for Christmas.

“Go up and talk to dispatch!” Beverly was firm. “I have no control over the loads and you know that!”

He jumped out of the truck and she followed him as he stomped into the terminal and up the stairs to the dispatch window. "Do you have a load for us yet?" he asked in a congenial voice.

She was shocked. "What happened to the vulgarity?"

They finally got a load that allowed them to stop at her family's home long enough to have Christmas dinner. He was livid. He sat in the jump seat cussing at her as she drove out of Ontario, California.

Beverly was a survivor of many types of abuse. She had learned at an early age to simply turn off reality. It was probably frustrating to a person when their verbal brutalization falls on deaf ears. Finally in New Mexico she asked him, "What are you yelling about?"

After a few moments of silence, "I can't remember," he said in amazement.

"Then it must be real important. Why don't you just go to the bunk so you're rested when it's your turn to drive?"

He never quit yelling at and demeaning her. He usually waited until she was driving and couldn't get away from him. A couple of months later she left him and the truck at the terminal.

"You can't leave me here," he pleaded as she was taking her stuff off the truck.

"I didn't take you to raise! This is where I picked up the truck and this is where I'm supposed to drop it!"

"But I love you!" he swooned.

"I don't want to be loved that way!" as she climbed out of the truck with what she could carry.

Beverly walked into the terminal and told the woman in the safety department that she was leaving.

"Is he a good driver?" she asked Beverly about her husband.

"He's a darned good driver, but he just sucks as a husband," Beverly said as she walked out of her office.

Beverly called a cab and went to the local truck stop. She took a shower, changed clothes, and called the safety department of her old company. She told them what had happened and that she was hitchhiking home. The head of the safety department told her to call him the next morning to see what he could find for her.

As Beverly sat on the bench inside the driver's door at the truck stop, hoping to find a safe driver to give her a ride home, she remembered feeling abandoned when Wendell drove off and left her on their first trip. She was lucky this time too because she caught a ride with a driver that had been to AA meetings. They connected on that level and he made sure that she didn't get hurt. She could have been a missing person like so many other women that just never come back from out there.

Beverly went back to work for her old company at a fuel stop in Kansas City. One of their driver's father had died and the team was on their way back to the terminal via Kansas City. They picked Beverly up and she rode back with them. They got off the truck at the terminal and she delivered their load. She got her own truck again when she got back to the terminal.

Beverly was still pondering her fate, "Yep that must be it. Other women put up with demeaning treatment. That must be the reason that men keep treating us that way then? Or maybe there are actually men that like their wives and treat them with love and respect. I know there are! Dad did! There, that's what I want! Someone that actually likes me…allows me to be the best I can be…understands when that isn't real good.

Okay, now that I know what I want, and what I've had, maybe it's time to see what I've been doing to get what I've been getting."

This part of Beverly's life started in the '80s. She was in the process of ending her forth marriage. She discounted men and regarded them as disposable. The reason she learned to do this will be the subject of another book. Let it suffice that she was able to survive lots of things with this attitude. She had watched other women be destroyed by a lot less.

Beverly would meet someone that treated her well, believe the nice things he told her, and marry him. Invariably everything would change and she would say to herself, "NOPE! This ain't the one!"

Beverly visualized herself as a filly, minding her own business, pulling a cart down the road. A stallion would come along and promise her a wonderful life if she would just help him pull his heavy wagon. She would believe him and hitch to his wagon. Everything would be all right for a while, but eventually the wagon would get harder to pull. She would look over and the stallion would be lying on the ground while she pulled him and the wagon. It happened time after time. She'd emotionally flip him over her shoulder, hitch herself back to her smaller wagon, and trot down the road.

Beverly had met Homer in an alcohol treatment facility. She had been sober for over five years and got drunk one night. She'd never been to treatment and thought that maybe it would be the answer. They told her to not make any changes or get into any relationships for a year, so naturally she married the nice man that she met there. She doesn't know if Homer ever quit drinking. She did. In fact, that was the last time, June 1981.

Beverly had closed her drapery shop, sold her house to Becky, and moved to a southern coastal city with Homer so he could take a new job. They moved back to Ted's house and then to another southern state.

Beverly lived through a couple years of being married to an active alcoholic because she really didn't want to fail at marriage. They were years of packing her things into a U-Haul trailer and going back to live with Ted for a few months; back to try it again with Homer who had promised to change; and back to Ted's because he hadn't.

On these trips Beverly would talk on the CB to truckers. One day someone said, "Hot Air, what are you driving?"

The answer simply came out by itself, "A 6-wheeler working my way up to an 18." The more she said it, the better it sounded.

After that divorce Beverly told Ted that she wanted to go to truck driving school. She doesn't think that it shocked him. She had always been a tom-boy on the farm and preferred working in the field or with the animals to doing housework, cooking, or sewing. She'd learned to do all of those things, but she loved the freedom of the outdoors and she will never forget how proud she was the first time he let her drive the tractor by herself.

Ted handed Beverly a check for $1,000 and she enrolled in a truck driving school in the city. She learned to herd a 9-speed, single bunk cab-over with no power steering or air conditioning at that school. She pulled around an empty 45-foot trailer. She can't tell you that she learned to drive a truck there because there's a big difference between herding it and driving it!

Beverly almost laid the truck on its side the first time she drove. "You slow this damn thing down! If the trailer would have been loaded, we'd be laying back there in the ditch!" Willie, her instructor, yelled at her. He was still bracing himself for her next move.

She got the truck herded out onto the interstate and asked, "Can I smoke?" ignoring his obvious horror.

"Can you smoke and keep it on the road at the same time?" he mused as he relaxed his grip on the hand bracket that's usually used to climb into the truck.

Beverly owes Willie a lot. They laughed a lot while he was teaching her. All except when she was backing that piece of crap up. It was in the summer; hot, humid, and no wind. The fan between the visors sometimes worked, but it did little for the humidity. She would sweat, work at turning the wheel with no power steering, first one way and then the other, and finally yell out the window at Willie seated on a retaining wall and reading his daily paper. "I hate this fucking truck!"

He wouldn't even look up. "You'll appreciate a good one when you get into it. Now back it into the hole."

Later, Beverly learned that it's easier to turn the wheel while the truck's moving, whether she had power steering or not. She also learned that there's no way to teach someone to back a truck up. The only way is to get into it and do it. As in many other aspects of life, experience is the only teacher.

Willie was an over-the-road truck driver. He knew these things. He'd gotten a few too many speeding tickets "out there" and was teaching at the school while time ran out and his license was clean again. He told Beverly, "You can lose your license for good if you get too many tickets." She heard that he went back out driving after she left school, but she never ran across him.

The first day of classes Beverly told Willie, "I want you to teach me the real stuff. None of this crap that you're supposed to teach us."

He just smiled, turned, and said, "Get in the truck."

Beverly thinks he was harder on her than the others because he knew how badly she wanted to go over-the-road. He made her drive through construction areas that she just knew the truck wouldn't fit through…it did…most of the time.

"You didn't even look in your mirror to see where your trailer was!" Willie yelled at Beverly one day. "You almost hit that construction worker!"

"How in the hell am I supposed to look in my mirror and out the windshield at the same time? There were construction workers in front of me, too, ya know!!" she yelled back.

"Just do it!" He shook his head with disgust.

Later that day, he took Beverly aside, "Look, Bev, driving a truck isn't like driving a car. To do the job right you have to keep your eyes moving. You have to know what's in front of you, where your trailer is, where other vehicles are around you, what your gauges are telling you at any given moment, and how the engine is sounding. You have to become one with your truck."

Only experience and practice could really teach Beverly what he was insisting that she learn that day. To be truthful about it, she doesn't think she really felt it until she was driving solo a few years later. As long as she was a second seat she could always defer to the first seat. Only by forcing herself to do the complete job did she understand what Willie was trying to tell her.

Willie taught Beverly some of the terminology that she would need to know. "The two front tires on the tractor are called the steers and the set of eight tires on the back of the tractor is called the drives because you turn the front ones to steer the truck and the others power the truck down the road; hence drivers."

Beverly thought that made sense.

Then he told her, "The set of eight tires on the trailer are called the tandems."

"Why?"

"Because tandem means close-coupled pairs of axles." He went on as she opened her mouth, "Yes, the drives are also tandems, but dispatch and the mechanics like to know which set we're talking about when we call in for repairs so we call them different things."

How did he know what she was going to ask?

As the days went by, Willie directed Beverly's attention to different parts of different trucks, "A cab-over has a flat front on the tractor. The entire cab sits on top of the motor. There's a doghouse between the seats, because a dog can sit there and see out the windshield. A single-bunk has a mattress that is narrower than a single bed, a double-bunk in a cab-over has a mattress that is between a double and queen sized mattress. A double bunk in a long-nose tractor means that there are two bunks in the sleeper, one above the other."

He continued her lessons, "A long-nose or conventional tractor has the motor out in front of the cab. They can have a single, double, or sit-in bunk. A stand-up, walk-in bunk usually has two bunks."

Beverly looked puzzled. "What's a sit-in?"

"That's where there's no floor space between the bunk and the cab. You simply stand between the seats, turn around, and sit down on the bunk," he explained. "The stand-up, walk-in conventional Pete is the most desired and most comfortable for the driver. That's what I have." He had pride in his voice.

"What's that?"

"It's a Peterbuilt tractor that has room to stand up in front of the bunk to put your pants on," he mused. "You have to lie down in the bunk of the cab over to pull them on."

Willie taught her that there are different engines, "There's the CAT, the Cummins, the Detroit, and the Mack. They come in all sizes."

"Why?"

He was patient. "Because each job needs a different size motor. If you drive in the mountains, you'll need a bigger motor than if you just drive around Iowa. If you're pulling heavy loads, you need a bigger motor than if you only haul light loads like crackers."

"Which type is the best?"

"That's up to each driver." He laughed. "You'll hear arguments every day in the truck stops and on the CB about that one! The less you know, the better off you'll be out there."

Beverly adopted the dumb truck-driver's attitude that day. She also added female to the front of it. It worked to get her out of a few over-weight, log violation, and speeding tickets in the years to come.

Learning to do log books was interesting to say the least. You see, the Department of Transportation has rules that drivers are supposed to follow. They're probably real good rules, too, but the only way a driver makes any money is if the wheels on their truck are turning. Shippers, receivers, brokers, and dispatchers really don't care how the driver does it, but what they don't want to hear is, "I've run out of hours on my log." Beverly tried it one time.

The dispatcher said, "So start another book!" and hung up on her.

Willie told her, "You learn the legal way to do logs for now. You're smart enough to figure out the rest later. If not, ask somebody to help you."

Finally, the day came that Beverly and several other students were going to take their driving test to get their chauffeur's license. Willie told them, "Now remember, when you're going out onto the street, don't stop traffic from either direction! Just sit there and wait! He's flunked other students right there."

When it was Beverly's turn, she pulled the truck around, stopped and waited for traffic to clear from both directions. Finally she said to the examiner, "Do ya wanna do lunch?"

He smiled, the traffic finally cleared, and she started maneuvering the truck as he requested. The test went like a breeze and he told Willie that she was the best driver he'd brought him so far.

"You flirted with him, didn't you?" Willie mused.

"Maybe…"

"You're going to do all right out there!" He sounded sad. "Just don't let 'em burn ya out."

Beverly had no idea what he was trying to tell her. She was to learn through the next few years just how vicious it can be for a woman on the road. She is sure Willie hoped she would have enough sense to park the truck when she was too tired to drive it, since he was always harping on it, but she didn't actually learn to say no until after she started driving solo.

It was a tradition for students to take Willie to lunch on the day they got their license. Of course, it was Willie that started that tradition, but Beverly thought it was a good idea. After all, he'd put his life on the line every time he climbed into the truck while she was driving.

They had lunch at one of those buffet places. You know the type, lots of food, some of it eatable. When they got back to the school, "Beverly!" the president of the school grabbed her arm, "A driver for a west coast company called while you were gone and asked if we have any female students that want to drive over-the-road. I told him that you do and he'll be here in about an hour to see if you want to drive with him."

"Cool!" she said and gave Willie a questioning look.

"They are a good company to drive for," Willie told her. "As for this particular driver, you'll have to figure that out on your own. Just remember that you'll be intimately together 24-7. There isn't a lot of room to get away from each other in a truck."

Just then a beautiful dark blue double-bunk Kenworth cab-over drove into the driveway. There was something on the front of the trailer that sounded like a motor running real fast, "Willie, what's on the front of his trailer?"

"Oh shit," Willie snapped his fingers, "I didn't teach you about reefers did I? Well, just remember to defrost it often, even in the winter. He'll teach you the rest."

Beverly supposes that you could call that day the beginning of her boy-toy phase. Her third husband had been eleven years older than her. The rest had been two to five years her senior. This hillbilly was 31-years-old; nine years younger. She had always heard that life would begin at forty.

Beverly stood there in the driveway and watched him climb down out of the truck. He was 6' 4" tall, lanky, and played the dumb hillbilly truck driver role to the hilt that day. "Hi! I'm Wendell."

Willie introduced them and asked what his company was paying. Beverly can't remember for sure but she thinks it was nineteen or twenty one cents a mile split between the team. Of course, the first seat got the extra penny.

Willie asked about insurance, pickup and drop pay. After they'd talked for awhile Willie gave Beverly the nod and left her there to fend for herself.

"Do ya wanna come look at the inside of the truck?" Wendell said shyly, "I had ta clean it out fore you saw it. Drivin' by myself don't leave time for housekeepin'."

"Sure!" Beverly was eager to see what a real truck looked like on the inside. It was beautiful dark blue with the company logo in white lettering on the door. The trailer was white with the same logo in blue stretched down each side. The inside of the tractor was blue vinyl and the bunk was huge.

There was a closet and a couple of shelves at the foot of the mattress. Wendell told Beverly that he had to buy queen-sized sheets, "Cuz the double ones ain't bignuff for this mattress."

His sheets looked like the jungle in brown and beige hues. He had a correlating brown velour blanket spread on top and king-sized pillows with the same animal print leaning on the walls around the mattress. There was a cabinet on the back wall above the mattress that really impressed her that day. Later, after she had hit her head on it a few times trying to sit up, it lost its appeal.

After Wendell and Beverly climbed back out of the tractor he showed her the storage in the side boxes that could only be accessed from the outside the tractor. Then, "We have tank heaters ta keep the fuel warm in the winter, a air-dryer to keep the moisture outta the air lines so they don't freeze in the winter, and adjustable fifth wheel that connects the trailer to the tractor and moves forward or backwards ta distribute the weight instead of climbin' into the trailer and movin' the cargo."

Beverly thought to herself, *Does he think I'm an idiot? Willie taught me that!*

Wendell was still talking, "We can't move the tandems on the trailer though, they're welded. I guess other drivers didn't know what they were doin and ruined a few trailers; pulled the trailer clean off the wheels."

"Okay," Beverly said excitedly, "when do we leave? I have to do some laundry. I wasn't expecting to leave today."

"Ahhhh," there goes that cute southern drawl again, "I dunno for sure that the company'll hire ya."

Beverly was shocked! She had never considered that a company wouldn't hire her, and she certainly hadn't thought that maybe a man wouldn't want to drive with her. He told her later, "I thought you were a bit pushy."

Beverly wasn't ready to give up. "Well, if you want," she said, "you can follow me out to my dad's and park on the frontage road by his house while we take our laundry in town. We can talk while it's washing and drying."

"Yea, I guess." He started toward the truck.

Beverly looked in the rear-view mirror most of the way to Ted's. She imagined what it would be like to be sitting in the driver's seat of that big beautiful truck. She smiled to herself. "He doesn't know it, but he just got a partner!"

Wendell backed the truck down the frontage road. Beverly went inside the house and grabbed her laundry, skipped back outside, and pulled the car over in front of the tractor. He climbed out of the cab with a pillow case full of dirty clothes and got into the car.

On the way to the laundromat they compared their families. They each had one brother and one sister. Wendell was the oldest and Beverly was the middle child. His father was dead and her mother had been killed in a car accident with her daughter. He had no children and she refused to have any more because she never wanted to feel that much pain again.

Wendell told her he'd learned to drive chip-trucks up and down the mountains of West Virginia and Virginia. "It's similar to the logging trucks on the west coast 'cept the mountains are shorter and faster on the east side. That's awl we do and we're damned good at it!" he told her with his puffed-out hillbilly chest.

Beverly knew that he was watching her while she loaded the machines. She also knew that he apparently liked what he saw or he wouldn't have followed her for over twenty miles to have this talk. "So where does your company send you?"

"We run the continental forty-eight, plus Canada." He was sitting on the edge of a table used to fold clothes. "They keep me movin' so much I just can't do it by myself any more. I'm lookin' for someone that'll stay out there with me."

"That's the reason I went to school," Beverly said, "so I could go long-haul."

He tilted his head. "Do ya really wanna be gone from home all the time?"

"Look," she sighed, "I just got a divorce. My ex-husband changed the locks on our apartment and kept everything that I'd accumulated. Home for me is a bedroom at my dad's house."

"You'll hafta hide in the bunk when we cross the coups until they hire ya," he warned.

"What's the coups?"

He looked puzzled. "The weigh stations."

"Oh, why do I have to hide?"

"'Cause you ain't s'pose ta be on my truck. The company insurance won't cover ya 'til you're hired and I could git fired if they find ya."

"So I'll hide!"

There was a long moment of silence. Beverly could tell that he was sizing her up. "Let's do it!" He smiled for the first time. They finished the laundry, went back to the truck, climbed into the cab, closed the doors, and started their life together on the road.

There has to be organization inside of a truck. Space is at a premium. Everything has to be in its place or the drivers feel closed in. Each one has to have their own amount of space or they feel cramped. Just as a driver becomes one with the truck and can feel its dimensions, he or she also, in time, becomes one with their partner; anticipates rather than asking questions.

Beverly lived on Wendell's pay advances that trip to California. The dispatchers didn't know there were two of them in the truck so there were lots of excuses made for the need for extra money.

Wendell drove out of town that day with Beverly in the jumpseat. She watched as he grabbed gears and rolled off the hills in western Iowa. She shuddered when he got closer to the 4-wheelers in Omaha than she thought he should. Then on the west side of Lincoln, "Do ya wanna try it?" he asked me.

"Drive?"

"Yea, that's the reason I called the school. I'm beat!"

"Sure!"

He pulled off on the shoulder and started lecturing her, "Don't EVER pull off on the shoulder less you absolutely have to! 'Specially at night. Drivers are tired and will hit the back of yur trailer thinkin' that yur still movin'. Always put yur flashers on when the truck is goin slow or is stopped less yur in a truck stop, and ALWAYS use yur flashers when yur backin' up!" Beverly's lessons had started.

Wendell crawled into the bunk, threw a pillow on the dog-house, situated himself on his stomach and one elbow. "Well, Darlin, let's see if ya can get this thing a movin'."

Beverly smiled at him and crawled over the dog house into the drivers seat. She moved the seat up and forward to fit her 5' 7" body, reached out the window and moved the mirror so she could see beside the trailer, and looked in the right mirror. Wendell was already coming out of the bunk to position the right mirror for her. This became a process that they went through every time they changed drivers until they bought the electric mirror for the rider's side.

Beverly pushed in the clutch and the brake, put the truck in gear, released the parking brakes, turned on the left turn signal, looked in the left mirror, and started rolling down the shoulder. She gained speed and grabbed gears until the traffic cleared so that she could move out into the lane and finally made it to the big hole/top gear.

Beverly had never felt such power under her before. She'd never pulled a loaded trailer before. For the first time she realized that she was heading into the open spaces of Nebraska with a complete stranger.

Beverly's not really sure when Wendell went to sleep. She had the radio and the CB both on. All she knows is that she started to say something to him and he'd dropped the curtain between the bunk and cab. She assumed then, and learned for sure later that it meant, "Leave me alone."

The drag of the loaded trailer was offset by the larger engine in the tractor. It had a 9-speed transmission like the one Beverly had learned on, but the rpms dropped faster than they had with the empty trailer so she had to grab the gears in a different way. By the time she had gone through them a few times on level ground she felt fairly confident.

The sun was shining, other drivers were flirting with Beverly on the CB, country western was mellow on the stereo and she was happy. The only thing she knew for sure is that she was supposed to stop at Big Springs…wherever that was. She finally found it that evening. She pulled into the truck stop, found a parking place, and set the brakes. She pulled the bunk curtain aside. "Wendell, we're in the Big Springs truck stop."

"Okay."

"I'm going in to use the restroom." She grabbed her purse and climbed down to the ground.

He yelled after her, "Yea, I'll meet ya in the restaurant. I hafta fuel so it'll be awhile."

Beverly used the rest room and walked back out to the fuel island where Wendell had moved the truck. "Can I help with anything?"

"Yea, ya can wash off the bugs ya put on my windshield."

Beverly smiled, found the ladder on wheels, got the squeegee out of the solution, and commenced her part of the fueling process…she thought. Later they decided that the one that drove into the truck stop would do the fueling, check the oil, clean the windows and mirrors, and do the vehicle check to allow the other one time to wake up. This arrangement worked well for about three years.

After the truck was fueled and moved back to a parking spot, Wendell started lecturing Beverly at the dinner table. "Bev, ya need ta train yourself ta go ta sleep as soon as ya get in the bunk. We're gonna drive for five hours and be in the bunk for five hours. When we get goin', and ya learn the roads, I'll need ya to be ready to drive when my five hours are up." He looked at her to make sure that she was listening, "Ya go to bed after we git back in the truck and I'll wake ya up to show ya how ta go down Sherman."

"What's Sherman?"

It's a hill between Cheyenne and Laramie. It can git kinda tricky, specially in the winter. It ain't nothin if ya know what yer doin' though."

They finished their meal, visited the rest rooms, climbed into the truck, and Beverly crawled into the bunk. "Good night," she said as he dropped the curtain between the bunk and cab.

It was mostly dark with a small amount of light coming around the edges of the curtain. She looked around the bunk and thought it looked like a big coffin. She wondered why she didn't feel claustrophobic. Instead, it felt more like the safety of the womb. Of course, she couldn't actually remember what the womb felt like, but it felt secure anyway.

The curtain was pulled aside and Wendell came crawling into the bunk. "Here, let me show ya how ta sleep in a bunk." He put a king-sized pillow on each side of her and one under my head. "This way ya won't be rollin all over the place. If I have ta stop fast, ya won't come rollin out on the doghouse."

"Thanks, I feel so pampered!"

"Oh," Wendell continued, ignoring her remark, "I forgot ta tell ya. If I'm not in the truck and ya have to get out, always put a pillow in the driver's seat so I'll know yur not in the bunk. One driver I know drove off and left his wife at the truck stop. She got out to use the rest room and had to have the police catch him so she could get back in the truck." He laughed. "I don't wanna go through the tongue lashin' he said he got!" He kissed Beverly on the forehead and smiled into her eyes. "Goodnight, darlin'." He crawled back out into the cab.

It was like being rocked in a cradle. Okay, sometimes a rocking cradle in an earthquake, but Beverly fell asleep feeling happy and secure.

Wendell woke Beverly up to show her how to go down Sherman and she stayed up for awhile to watch how he used the gears over Elk Mountain. He showed her how to go through the canyons into Salt Lake City and explained why they didn't go over Parley, "We don't have a jake and we're loaded pretty heavy. It's just safer to go this way. Besides, you hafta learn to drive through canyons while there ain't no snow or ice on the roads. Gits a bit tricky when that stuff comes."

Beverly drove to Wendover, Nevada. That was the first time she told God about his lack of creativity in that part of the country, "Were you on a coffee break or something when you made the salt flats?"

Wendell got back in the driver's seat and showed Beverly how to grab gears climbing hills, and told her which hills not to roll off of. He taught her which gear to be in at the top of a steep down grade and which gauge to watch on the way down, "If ya git the brakes smokin', and they git hot enough, you don't have no brakes and no way to stop the truck."

Wendall was young and rolled off of some hills that Beverly downshifted for. He had more experience and told her, "You always drive the truck so yur comfortable. Don't listen ta anybody else when they try ta getcha ta take chances! Ya always keep this truck under control and don't listen to anybody on the CB. You have our lives in yur hands when yur behind the wheel. I won't hurt you and you don't hurt me. You know what yur capable of. They don't! They'll git us killed!"

Beverly doesn't think that she ever rolled off of a hill without thinking to herself, *I wonder what would happen if one of these steering tires blew*. She guesses that probably made it more exciting because she didn't stop doing it.

Actually, the only time she ever blew a steering tire, she was going up a steep grade and it was no problem stopping the truck. It was, however, a problem for the repairman to maintain the tractor safely on the jack while the tire was being replaced.

Beverly drove into Sparks, Nevada. Wendell had told her to pull into the 76 truck stop and park at the fuel island. She pulled the curtain aside. "Wendell, we're here."

"Okay, hit the rest room and I'll fuel."

"Okay!" She grabbed her purse and hit the ground running. She'd had to go for quite awhile by then and he wasn't going to get an argument from her.

He fueled, they took a shower, ate dinner, and went back to the truck. "We're gonna stay here tonight," he told Beverly.

"Okay," she said as she climbed into the bunk. She changed into her sleep-shirt and waited for him. They had a passionate sexual encounter.

He told her, "I won't get married again 'til I meet somebody who gets me off orally."

She smiled at him. "No problem!" She drifted off to sleep.

The next morning, Beverly woke with an urgency to use the rest room. "Wendell, I've gotta go really bad!"

"Okay, get dressed and we'll go inside."

Beverly got dressed and climbed into the jump seat. The cab-over across the isle was whipping its antennas back and forth like a dog shaking water from its head. "Wendell, what's the matter with that truck?"

He stuck his head out the curtain, looked in the direction she was pointing, and started laughing. He really started laughing when she realized that that was what their truck had looked like the night before. "You mean?"

"Yep!"

They laughed and started bonding as friends that day.

Wendell drove when they left Reno for Sacramento. "You need ta stay up and watch now, Bev. Do ya remember the Donner Pass thing?"

"Yea, isn't that where people ate each other to survive the winter?"

"Yep, we're bout to go over that hill now."

She smiled at him. He did a double-take. "No, we ain't stoppin' on top!" he said with a business tone in his voice. "Ya need to learn how ta drive this hill!"

She pouted a little, but truck driving reality was sinking in. There was little time for fun. Wendell taught her that their first responsibility was to get the load picked up and delivered on time. He told her that he had the reputation of being a runner and he wanted the company to depend on them to do the same.

"There's the Truckee coup," Wendell quipped. "Jump in the bunk and close the curtain. California don't like truckers. They want us to bring em what they want in their stores and take their produce back, but they really don't want us hangin around their state. They'd just love ta find ya in my truck."

"Why? What did we do to them?" Beverly crawled into the bunk and closed the curtain.

"Well, one of our drivers took a couple construction workers off the side of this hill with him awhile back. All three of 'em died."

"He didn't do it on purpose, did he?"

"Naw, the whole story hasn't come out yet. It don't matter, though. Any time a big truck is involved in anything, it's automatically the driver's fault."

Wendell drove through the scales and back out onto the road. Beverly climbed back into the jump seat.

After a few more miles he pulled off to the side where the shoulder usually was and parked. It was paved and other trucks were parked there, too. "Ya have ta stop here every time ya come over this hill, Bev. Ya need to get out and make sure that yur brakes ain't hot, ya don't have any air leaks, and nothin's wrong with yur truck. If the police catch ya not stoppin, they'll ticket ya."

"Why?" She realized that this must be serious stuff.

"We're gettin ready ta go down the west side of Donner. There's nothin ta be afraid of, but I wantcha to respect this hill! There's a couple good drops, but there's signs ta tell ya what ta do."

Beverly thinks that was the first time that her orifices really tightened up on her. She could tell that Wendell respected this hill more than the others. She'd watched him coming down Sherman and Elk, but he had an entirely different attitude about Donner.

Beverly watched as he explained which gear to be in when she started down the hill and which gauge to watch to make sure that the brake pressure was correct. "Once ya put yur brakes on at the top, don't let up on em til yur ready to stay off em for awhile. Air brakes are different than car brakes. If ya pump em, they get hot and start smokin'. If ya get em hotnuff, they glaze. Then ya don't have any brakes at all. If that ain't bad nuff, they can catch on fire and burn up your trailer and load. Dispatch gets REEEL upset about that one."

"Okay," Beverly said, letting him know that he definitely had her attention, "you're not going to make me drive over this for awhile, are you?"

He actually laughed again. "Probly not."

Beverly never saw Wendell smoke his brakes. He was a real stickler about making sure they were adjusted in Utah so they'd be seated by the time they got to California. He did the same thing if they were going to southern California because, "Cajon and Tehachapi can git a little tricky, too," he told her several times.

They finally got to Sacramento. They stopped at the 76 truck stop and had breakfast. Then they were off to make their first delivery. Beverly doesn't remember how many drops they had, but she remembers arriving at Bakersfield after they finished.

"I'm gonna drop ya off here at the truck stop," Wendell was telling Beverly as he drove into the parking lot. "Here's money for the cab and the address of the terminal. Ya call the safety department and tell 'em that yur on yur way in ta take yur drivin' test. I've already talked to 'em 'bout ya bein' my partner."

Beverly felt abandoned as Wendell drove off leaving her standing in the parking lot with her suitcase. By the look on his face he was feeling the same thing. She walked into the building, called the number on the paper, and asked for the safety department. "Where are you?" a male voice asked.

She tried to sound confident, "I'm at the 76 truck stop here in Bakersfield. I can catch a cab over there if it's all right."

"Sure, just ask for me."

She hung up and called for a cab. She felt vulnerable standing there waiting. The leers and nasty remarks from the dirty, fat, ugly drivers when they walked by forced her to vow that she'd never allow herself to be in this position again.

Beverly climbed into the cab and told the driver where she wanted to go. When they got to the terminal she saw lots of trucks just like the one Wendell had brought her to California in. Some of them were single bunks, but they were all the same beautiful blue.

She paid the cab driver and carried her suitcase into the building.

A nice young woman escorted her to the safety department and introduced her, "This is the head of the safety department."

"Well," he got up from his chair and started toward the door of his office, "it's going to take your partner all day to catch his log books up. I'll get you started on your paperwork after we see if you can drive."

They walked out of the building to the parking lot and climbed into a different truck than she had been driving. "Do you know which pedal the brake is?" he asked.

She was shocked! "Yea, the middle one. Why?"

"Okay, you can start the truck then," he said in a monotone voice.

She didn't move. She just sat there and looked at him.

He chuckled. "The last person that climbed into that seat asked me which pedal was the brake. I told him to get out of my truck. Since you know where the brake is, you can start the truck."

She chuckled, too, shook her head, and started the truck. She probably wouldn't have been able to pass that test if Wendell hadn't taught her how to drive in the mountains. The safety manager had her climb Tehachapi and come back down. She didn't learn how to do that in Iowa because Iowa doesn't have any mountains like that.

They talked during the test. She told him about her divorce, going to truck driving school, and Wendell calling to see if there was a female that wanted to drive over-the-road with him. He didn't ask her how she got to California and she didn't offer the information. He told her that he'd been an over-the-road driver for over twenty years so she figured they both knew what had happened.

They walked through the driver's room on the way back to the safety department. Wendell gave Beverly a questioning look and she shrugged her shoulders. The safety manager told Wendell, "You'd better get going on those logs Bud! Your partner'll be ready to roll in about an hour. Dispatch has a hot load for you two and you're not leaving here until your logs are brought up to date!"

All of them smiled and Beverly was handed form after form, test after test, and then she had to pee in a bottle. She still doesn't understand why someone can't come up with a larger mouthed bottle for females to hit. She thinks it is probably "when in Rome."

Wendell finally got his logs done that evening. He told Beverly, "You learned how ta do these damned logs in school, didn't ya? Make 'em look good." She would fill in the lines and he'd sign his sheet. She also was put in charge of doing the paperwork, keeping the inside of the truck clean, the laundry, and keeping the refrigerator filled. He took care of the outside of the truck; kept the brakes adjusted and did any repairs that needed to be done on the road.

Their first trip was to Toledo, Ohio. They both took pride in being labeled "runners". That meant that dispatch knew that they wouldn't be playing around in Nevada, or stopping any more than necessary. They showered once a day when they fueled, sat down for a meal if we had time, and only stopped for short pit-stops along the road. Many times they would slip-seat (*switch drivers while continuing down the road*), instead of taking time to stop the truck.

Dispatch didn't have a load back out of Toledo that first time. Beverly supposes they didn't know what to expect from her, but they always had one waiting for them after that. They didn't sit very often.

Wendell got a motel room for the weekend after they delivered their load in Toledo. Then they met other drivers from their company in the bar. Beverly danced, played pool, and drank soda pop. Wendell drank everything alcoholic that he could find! He took half-full glasses back to the room and left them sitting all over the place. About midnight she helped him back to the room and watched as he wilted on top of the covers. She walked around the room and picked up the plastic glasses of booze, poured them down the drain, and rinsed out the sink. She got into bed on the opposite side from him and kept her face turned away from him. You see, she had been sober for a few years by that time and booze breath really made her sick to her stomach.

The next morning Wendell woke with a terrible hang-over. "Ya CAN'T be a alcoholic!"

"What are you talking about?" Beverly was shocked.

"Ya told me yur a recovering alcoholic. If ya were, ya'd have drunk the booze I left sittin' round the room stead of pourin' it all down the sink."

"You'd better hope that I poured it out, bud! Don't you EVER test me like that again!" She swatted his shoulder with her hand.

About a month later he decided Beverly should back the trailer up. They were picking up a load in California and there were no other trucks on the lot; six empty doors and the shipper had said, "Just pick one."

"Okay darlin', put it in any hole ya want ta," as Wendell climbed down to the ground.

Do you remember how much Beverly liked backing the truck up when she was in truck driving school? Well, this one was bigger and the trailer was longer. She pulled forward, jack-knifed the tractor against the wire fence, and stopped. She looked out the window to see the 6'4" hillbilly jumping up and down like Yosemite Sam. She was sure she saw smoke coming out of his ears, too! "Maybe you'd better put it in," she told him, trying not to laugh.

It wasn't amusing to Wendell. He climbed into the cab, slammed the door, ground the transmission into reverse, and almost spun the tires. He backed up, hit the dock with the trailer and bounced off. He slammed the trailer back against the pads, set the brakes, jumped down to the ground, and stomped back to the tandems to set the chocks.

Beverly tried to explain and make up with him. "Willie never taught me how to back it up from that position. He only taught me how to jack-knife it into a dock."

Wendell wasn't buying it. She went to the tractor, climbed in, did her housecleaning, and brought their logs up to date. Later he told her, "I'll NEVER teach ya ta back the truck up, ya won't need me if ya know how!"

Beverly's mind went, *Oh yeah?*

She started paying more attention to the placement of the tractor and trailer before he started to back into places. She waited until he was asleep and practiced straightening the truck up in pull-through parking spaces. It just didn't make sense to her until an owner-operator told her, "Bev, it's simple to straighten it up. If you see your trailer in your right mirror, turn the wheel in that direction and your trailer will straighten out. If you see your trailer in your left mirror, turn the wheel in that direction to straighten it up. If you want to jackknife it, turn it in the opposite direction from the mirror you see the trailer in."

From that moment on she could back the truck up. She would set the brake so that she could get out and check her blind side because she didn't want to hit anything. She practiced and looked stupid until she could put the trailer where she wanted it to go. She'd walk on to the dock and ask the warehouse people, "Okay, who won the bet on how many times I'd have to pull up before I got it into the dock?" Most of the time she was usually assured that she had done a better job than some.

Dispatch sent Wendell and Beverly to New Jersey that first month too. They got to the receiver the night before their delivery time and Wendell let her sleep the next morning while he unloaded. She woke up when she felt the truck being backed into a parking space, come to a stop, and heard the brakes set. The curtain pulled aside, "Come on, darlin', let's get some breakfast."

"Where are we?"

"We're at what passes for a truck stop in New Jersey," he said sarcastically.

Beverly got dressed and crawled into the jump seat. The parking lot was deeply rutted dirt and the trucks were crammed together in spaces that would have been more appropriate for covered wagons. They got out of the truck and walked across to the small, dirty building.

Beverly opened the door to the women's rest room and started breathing through her mouth like she used to do in the outside toilet when she was growing up. Luckily she had also learned to squat instead of sitting on the seat. It was one of those places that made her skin crawl and feel dirty.

The eating area was filthy and Beverly suddenly had a craving for the food in their refrigerator. Wendell explained, "This place don't look like much, but we can git bout anything we want here, even a load if we have the money ta pay for it."

"The only thing I want is to leave!" she whispered.

He smiled, "Go call dispatch and tell 'em that we're empty, where we are, and that ya wanna get the hell outta here."

That was the first time that he'd allowed her to talk to dispatch. She ran to the phone. The dispatcher said, "Call back in an hour." That pattern repeated itself all day. By evening she wasn't understanding and patient any more. "You aren't going to leave me in this pigsty all night, are you?"

"Just a minute." He put her on hold. "Okay, do you have a pen?"

"Yes."

"Tell Wendell that I want you two at (*whatever truck stop he moved them to*)." All she remembers for sure is that they got to leave there and only went back one other time, also during the day.

There weren't a lot of female drivers in 1985. Not even driving team with their husband. Truck stops were mostly small, dirty, out-of-the-way places that had fairly good food and no shower facilities for women. Female drivers were mostly treated the same as lot-lizards (*female prostitutes that hung around the parking lots of truck stops and rest areas*).

Even the 76 truck stops had separate showers for women, and the 76s were about as good as there was at that time. An attendant would escort Beverly to the back of the building and open the door so she could enter the dimly lit, dirty shower room. After her shower she'd open the door to find a driver, sometimes two or three, outside waiting to proposition her for sex.

"I'm a driver!" she'd tell them.

"So? That don't mean you can't make some money on the side, does it?!"

She got pretty good at telling them, "Go fuck YOURSELF!" as she'd walk away.

Many of the laundry facilities were in the men's shower rooms. That meant, since Wendell had no idea how to separate clothes into colors, that they would unhook the tractor from the trailer and bobtail to a laundromat.

Beverly had been a regional loss-prevention secretary for a national corporation and was aware that the trucking company was getting a tax deduction for hiring her, other women and minorities. Affirmative Action gave them the same tax deduction for women as a black male. Beverly had a sense that female drivers would be listened to by management if they were unhappy and many of them voiced their grievances.

She talked to other women that drove team for their company when they'd meet on the road or at the terminal. They all started bitching to the safety department about the shower facilities at their required fuel stops. It wasn't long before the 76 truck stops started remodeling their shower facilities so that a team could shower in the same room. Laundry facilities were made accessible to women and the restaurants and rest rooms were cleaned up. Other truck stops followed in time.

Most of Wendell and Beverly's trips took them back and forth between California and Ohio or Pennsylvania. She didn't see the house for six weeks at a time and they very seldom got to Virginia so Wendell could visit his family.

One night Beverly was driving west. She had only been on the road for a few weeks. The driver that she had been talking to on the CB was turning south on a skinny road (*two-lane highway*), "You make it a good trip now, Hot Air," came over the CB as he made his exit.

"Thanks, is there a truck stop up here?" she asked. "I could sure use a cup of hot coffee."

"Yea, 'bout ten miles ahead of ya."

"I can probably make it that far. You make it a good trip, too."

"Later," was his departing word.

Beverly had observed that drivers seldom said goodbye to each other. The word "later" seemed to mean a lot of things; it's been good running with you, hope we run across each other again, have a good trip, etcetera. Of course, depending on the tone of voice it could also mean things like go away or you've gotta be kidding.

Beverly found the truck stop, parked, went inside to the rest room and bought a cup of coffee at the fuel desk. She walked back across the parking lot and climbed back into the driver's seat. A male voice came over the CB, "Are there any female drivers out there looking for a commercial buffalo (*a male prostitute*)?"

She looked at the speaker, smiled and shook her head. She wanted to play. She'd been behaving herself for far too long by this time and picked up the microphone. "How much do you want?" She put the truck in gear and started driving out of the lot.

"We'll have ta talk 'bout it," the same voice swooned.

"No! I've got a hot load, if you don't know how much it's worth, why should I be interested?"

"Oh I'm worth it, lady!" he assured.

"I've got a hundred dollars. What do I get for that?" she asked. She was on the big road (*interstate*) by then. The bunk curtain opened and Wendell stuck his head out; cleared his throat. "You finished now?"

Sheepishly she said, "Yea," and hung the microphone up.

Wendell told her later that the person in the bunk will wake up when the truck stops or makes an unnatural movement. She learned later that silence would also cause her to wake up. That meant they were on ice because the tires are silent on ice. Except, of course, when they're spinning out of control…that's a rude awakening, too!!

For whatever reason, known only to Wendell, he was a prolific liar. He'd tell people on the CB and in the truck stops that he was an owner-operator and that the truck was theirs. It seemed to her that he believed anything that he said. After a few months in the truck with him she realized that it's real hard to stay in reality when it's being distorted every day. Looking back, she supposes the drugs he took kept him in his own special world.

Driving team is worse than being married because you're together 24-7. Most married couples aren't together that much. Let me explain what it's like. Imagine that you and your mate go into your bathroom…no cheating now, the small one. The only time that you can come out is to eat a meal or go to the other rest room…for weeks at a time. See why they fought some?

Beverly woke up as the truck was stopping. She heard the brakes set. She pulled the curtain aside and looked through the windshield. They were parked at the fuel pump; 76 truck stop in a southern state. She got dressed, climbed into the jump seat, put on her shoes, climbed to the ground, and walked into the building. She went to the rest room, grabbed something to eat, and went back to the truck.

Wendell was talking with a very young girl, maybe 12-13. He said,

"This is (*whatever her name was*). She's gonna ride with us ta (*wherever she was going*)."

"Just a minute," Beverly said as she climbed into the truck and started packing her clothes.

"Whatcha doin'?" Wendell said as they climbed into the truck.

"I'm packing my clothes," she said nonchalantly. "Could you get on the CB and find me a ride?"

"Why? Ya don't have ta git off the truck."

"Oh yes, I do!" she was firm. "If she's going to ride with you, I'm going to need a partner that isn't going to get me fired for having a unauthorized, under-aged rider in the truck."

After a moment of silence Wendell told the girl, "I'm sorry. Ya gotta get out."

Young girls and boys were, and probably still are commodities on the road. About the only difference between living on the streets and living on the road is that people disappear easier on the road. They're held prisoner in the bunks of trucks until the driver gets tired of having them around. Then they're either dumped, given away or sold on the CB, or just simply disappear. There's a lot of space in the deserts and mountains of this country. How do I know this? Because every once in awhile one of them would escape while the driver was in the building. They'd go running across the parking lot naked, bruised, and bleeding.

Beverly had several bad experiences at a truck stop in a southern city. Once a waitress flung a plate of food on the table in front of her and the peas went flying. She sat Wendell's plate down with a smile. "There ya go, honey."

Beverly took her right hand and shot the plate back off of the table. It went skipping across the floor like a flat rock on a pond. "I'd like some food on my plate next time!"

The waitress apparently got the idea because the table and floor were wiped up and the next plate was carefully placed in front of her.

The next episode taught her that she might want to watch how she dressed. She and Wendell were running hard, but Beverly needed to get some laundry done. She told Wendell, "If you'll drive into the truck stop, I'll do the laundry and drive out while you sleep."

The bunk curtain opened. “Okay darlin’, we’re here. It’s my turn in there!”

Beverly could see the hot sun shining through the windshield so she put on her shorts and halter top, traded places with him, put on her three-inch slings and climbed out of the truck. She walked around to the rider’s door, opened it, and pulled out the bag of laundry.

As she started walking toward the building a man came running toward her, “I’ll give you $20 for a blowjob.”

She just looked at him. He waited a second. “Okay, $25.”

Still staring at him, she asked, “What truck do you drive?”

He pointed at an old single-bunk cab-over.

She pointed at theirs. “Do you see that one?”

“Yea?”

“I drive that one. Now if you want a blowjob, you get on the CB and ask someone else. But you leave me the hell alone!” *(I suppose this is probably cleaning up what she actually said, but you get the idea!)*

He sheepishly tucked what tail he had left and walked back in the direction of his truck. Beverly proceeded to do laundry, but she didn’t wear halter tops in parking lots after that unless Wendell was walking with her or she had another shirt over it.

Beverly started getting off of the truck every few weeks when they went through Iowa. Wendell would take the load to Toledo, or wherever it was going, and pick her up on his way back to California. She couldn’t understand why he got so upset about it. “After all, you’re going through here anyway,” she had told him. Later, when she started driving solo, she realized how hard it was on him to go back and forth between being a part of a team and driving solo.

The first time Beverly took one of these sabbaticals Wendell told her, “If ya don’t have jeans when I git back here, ya ain’t gittin’ back on the truck!”

Beverly hadn’t worn jeans since she was a teenager doing chores on the farm. She was now 40. She usually wore shorts or dress slacks, but she could tell that he meant it, so as much as she didn’t want to, she had five pairs of jeans when he came back for her.

Jeans were a big part of the driver's dress code then. Just as in any other vocation, everyone is supposed to go only so far in expressing themselves. Too much deviation is scorned. By the way, Beverly still has never owned a pair of cowboy boots like many of the other drivers were wearing at that time.

Years later when Beverly was driving solo, she had fueled at a truck stop in Illinois. She was standing at the fuel desk when a young man stopped next to her. She glanced and then did a double-take. He had on a big brown cowboy hat, a long brown leather cowboy duster over jeans and a plaid cowboy shirt. It was a fairly warm day and he really looked out of place. She rolled her eyes at the woman behind the desk and she smiled back. They both shook their heads because they knew he was getting the attention he wanted.

Beverly got her fuel receipt, walked back to the truck, and climbed in. She was sitting there getting her log book brought up when the same man walked back to the single-bunk cab-over sitting next to her. Her mouth dropped open when she saw the big silver spurs he was wearing. "I wonder what his floor mats look like," she said out loud. "It's a wonder he doesn't trip and kill himself climbing in and out of the truck."

A lot has changed, now many drivers are wearing sweats and running/walking shoes in lieu of the tight jeans and cowboy boots with leather soles that slipped on wet and icy surfaces. The one thing that doesn't change is the high status of driving a new truck.

Wendell and Beverly's company bought ten new International double-bunk cab-overs. The word spread that his top ten teams would get to drive them. Wendell and Beverly were ecstatic the day that they were told to move their stuff into one. There wasn't only high status for them as a team, there was also the responsibility to continue the same level of driving and on-time deliveries that had earned them the right to be one of the top teams.

Wendell had always kept the outside of the truck clean, polished, and chromed. Now he worked even harder at it. He bought long black mud flaps with chrome frames and chrome weights on the bottom. He decided to put chrome International logos in the middle of them because he didn't want to have a chrome woman on one of them and a chrome man on the other one. After all, Beverly had almost equal rights in the truck and if he was going to have a woman on one, then guess what!

He even bought an extra set of mud flaps for the trailer that matched the ones on the tractor. Wendell would exchange them for the generic company mud flaps when they switched to trailers.

Beverly had saved over $450 from her trip advances so that they could go to Disneyland and take a few days off. She was so excited. She'd been there right after it opened in the '50s and wanted to see how much it had changed. They stopped at the truck wash in Barstow on their way to L.A. There in the chrome shop was a black light bar for the back of the tractor. The clerk said, "There were only three of them made and only one black." It had eight tail lights and two backup lights. Wendell was actually petting it when Beverly walked in the door.

Does Beverly have to tell you that she still hasn't been back to Disneyland? Does she have to go into any detail about how beautiful it looked on their tractor? She would like to tell you that it was all Wendell's fault, but that would be a bold-faced lie. She enjoyed driving a Christmas tree (*shiny, lit-up, chromed-up truck*).

Wendell and Beverly got married in the park of her home town. Her family and friends were there. She would like to be able to tell you that their relationship was wonderful. It was a lot of the time. She would like to tell you that they lived happily ever after. What really happened was she is a recovering alcoholic and Wendell liked his drugs. They probably know each other better than anyone else will ever know them, at least the people they were then. Beverly hopes they both have grown up some since then.

Most of the time they simply ran back and forth across the country picking up and delivering loads. They drove hammer-down and didn't worry about tomorrow. Then there were the times that both of them should have been in *I-love-me-jackets*.

Wendell used to tell Beverly, "It really bugs me that ya don't git mad!"

Let me interpret that for you. "He's going to verbally pick at Beverly until she loses her temper. Then he can feel better because he's always mad about something."

Wendell never understood that machines break. Remember that beautiful light bar? Well, it used so many amps that it blew the flasher element to the point that he started stealing them from truck stops because they couldn't afford to keep replacing them. Circuit boards would actually have holes melted through them. Of course, it was the truck's fault, according to Wendell. He'd punch the truck until his hands would bleed.

One time the air conditioning quit. It was night and Beverly was driving eastbound on I-40. She doesn't remember exactly where she was because after awhile the interstate highways all blend into one long road. Anyway, she heard Wendell start cussing, screaming, and then crying from the bunk. Objects started hitting the walls. The curtain between the bunk and cab was torn off. Then he tore the curtain off the bunk window.

Beverly didn't say anything. She slowed the truck; drove up the exit, stopped for the stop sign, turned left and headed into the truck stop. She grabbed the CB microphone. "Is there a driver going to Iowa?"

Wendell grabbed it out of her hand and ripped it from the CB. "What the hell ya doin'?"

"I'm getting the hell out of this truck! Look at the mess you made back there! You think I want to drive with a NUT?!!!"

"Well, it's hot!"

"Wendell, most people get the air conditioner fixed!" She parked the truck, grabbed her purse, and jumped to the ground. She ran into the truck stop and hid in the women's rest room. She stayed in there for about an hour. Women kept coming in, "Are you, Beverly?"

"Yes?"

"There's a man outside the door. He said to tell you that Wendell isn't leaving without you, so you should just as well come out."

She finally got back on the truck, but he cleaned up the bunk first. "It'd better look like it did before you threw your tantrum, too!"

Beverly can't tell you that it was all Wendell though. One time they were arguing about something. All of the quarrels blended into one at some point. Anyway, this time he was driving and she was sitting in the jump seat. He pulled off on the shoulder to water the wheels (*urinate on the tires*). He stopped the truck, got out, and walked around the front of the truck and back to the drives that were away from traffic. Beverly was seething and watched him in the outside mirror. What happened next was, she is sure, caused by some demonic force. She opened the door just as he was hurrying past it.

He's 6' 4". Luckily, the door was curved on the bottom because it caught him in the middle of the forehead. He went screaming and bleeding into the ditch. She closed the door.

"I think it's time for me to go to the bunk," as she crawled across the doghouse, into the bunk, and closed the curtain.

Years later, when Wendell stopped to have coffee with her, she made her amends, "Wendell, do you remember when you ran into the door?"

"Yea, why?"

"I need to apologize to you. I opened the door on purpose."

"You BITCH! I KNEW IT!"

They both shook their heads and laughed. Beverly is sure that she had the same sad look on her face that he did, as they fondly remembered their years on the road.

Every person involved in this industry has their role and personal interests. The people who lease and sell the equipment are mainly interested in the industry's perpetual need for consumption. The company owners, office personnel, and mechanics want to maintain or increase their level of income. Law enforcement agencies try to make the industry accountable, but recognize they're only going to catch a small percentage of the drivers who are tired, drunk, or drugged.

Beverly can't forget the people who build, repair, and maintain the highways. Then add brokers, shippers, receivers, and lumpers (*day workers that are hired to load and unload cargo*), and you get some idea of the social interaction that a driver must successfully navigate. Since the goals of each job are usually in conflict with the goals of at least one other job on this list, tension exists constantly for a driver.

There's also the driving public. Their presence on the road impedes a driver's progress. Truck drivers aren't the only ones that need to learn about this profession.

Four-wheelers apparently have some uneducated assumptions about what a driver is capable of doing with 80,000 pounds that bends in the middle. Beverly had a friend tell her when she started truck driving, "You have all of those brakes, you can stop on a dime!"

"Yea, the one in your pocket!"

Common sense should tell everyone that 80,000 pounds traveling in excess of fifty miles an hour, most of the time a lot more than fifty miles an hour, will take longer to stop than 3,000 pounds traveling at the same speed.

Tailgating a truck seems to be a good idea for some reason to four-wheelers. Yes, staying close to the back of the trailer will probably save you some gas, but have you ever seen what the tread from a truck tire does when it goes through a windshield and impacts with a person's head?

It always made Beverly nervous when she knew that someone was so close to the back of her trailer that she couldn't see them in her mirror. She knew that if something happened and she had to break hard, the vehicle and driver would be imbedded in her trailer. She didn't want to walk back there afterwards. She did all of the things that she was taught; slow down, change lanes, speed up, hit the breaks and let up.

At times, it seemed the four-wheeler took pleasure in her attempts to get them off of her trailer. She began to see that the personalities of these people had to be similar to a small man who walks into a bar and for some reason can't help picking a fight with the biggest guy there.

Then there's the four-wheelers who seemed to think it was a good idea to pass trucks going down an icy hill, come over into their lane and hit their brakes. Beverly can't tell you how many times she helplessly looked into a child's eyes looking out of the back window, knowing that she couldn't stop.

You see, there's a lot more to driving a truck than simply jumping behind the wheel, learning to shift gears, and which pedal does what. A driver is responsible for freight that, combined with the weight of their tractor and trailer, weighs no more than 80,000 pounds.

To be legally distributed:

- steering axle: no more than 12,000 pounds
- drive axles (set): no more than 34,000 pounds
- trailer axles (set): no more than 34,000 pounds

Over-weight and over-length permits are usually obtained as needed.

The driver has to know how much fuel to put into the tractor so it doesn't exceed the legal gross weight crossing the next scale. This may also include snow, ice, or mud clinging to the vehicle.

The weight is distributed by moving the trailer tandems forward, which makes more of the trailer weight fall on them; or backwards, forcing the weight to the drives of the tractor. The same principle is true for moving the fifth wheel. Move it forward and the weight is thrown onto the steering tires; backwards and the steers are lightened. This takes experience, a math aptitude, and a grasp of distribution concepts.

Log books are a challenge if the driver is solo. It takes a mathematical genius and a good map if s/he's telling the truth, and even more talent to make a lie look good. The new technologies law enforcement and DOT have at their disposal are making it more difficult to make the logs match manifests, fuel receipts, and DOT checks. A driver usually has a choice to either be legal on their log or get the load delivered on time.

Some drivers back their log books up (*claim they started before they actually did*). Others fill out numerous logs and hope they hand the right one to the officer. They either log five hours on-duty and five hours off-duty or ten hours on-duty and eight hours off. Either way is legal as long as the entries allow the driver to be in their present location. (*New DOT regulations are different than when Beverly was driving.*)

When Beverly started driving she ran with the old-timers. They're the men and women who'd been driving for over twenty years. She would tell them she was new and asked them to tell her the most important thing that she should know about the job. At first, most of them just told her to go home. When they realized she was serious, they gave her wonderful advise:

"Expect every four-wheeler to make one mistake everyday, and expect it to be in front of your truck. You'll never be disappointed. You almost have to watch out for 'em since they don't seem capable of watchin' out for themselves."

"Drive your truck so you're comfortable. Don't ever let anybody tell you that you're not going fast enough. It's better to git there late than not git there at all."

"Don't be afraid to admit you made a mistake. We all make 'em and try to learn from 'em."

"Take care of your truck. Learn to listen to it and become part of it. It'll sing to you on those lonely nights and cry for help if you'll listen."

"Respect the big hills (*mountains*), you'll only make a mistake once on 'em."

"Never sign for a load that you haven't counted onto your trailer yourself. Always cover yur ass. Write 'shipper load and count' with your name."

There weren't very many women who could claim that amount of experience then, but the ones she found told her:

"Learn to back the truck up or you'll always be a second seat."

"Don't let anybody tell you that you can't do this job if that's what you want to do! But learn to do the whole job. Be a driver that we all can be proud of, not a crybaby when it gets rough out here. Go home if that's all you want."

"Always back into the trailer before you pull out from a parking space. A lot of men resent us being out here and will pull the pin so your trailer will fall on the ground and they can laugh at how stupid you are."

"Don't be afraid to ask for help. Your truck and load are more important than your pride."

"Don't dress, act or talk like a man. Be respected for your driving ability."

Socialization of the novice is supposed to take place in the truck driving schools. They advertise big money, lots of excitement, adventure, and secure incomes. They simply don't represent this lifestyle realistically. Driving isn't glamorous. Its dirty work, long hours, road construction, and the only respect you can expect is from other drivers, and that's only if your ability warrants it.

Usually its wind-driven rain, mud, snow, and sleet while you're fueling; checking the oil, water, and hoses, or the fuel jells and you're stranded in the middle of nowhere in minus 70 degree wind-chill. There's always freezing fog or snow is blowing so hard that you can't see the road in front of your tractor. Then its over 100 degrees in the shade, your air conditioner quits and dispatch says, "Keep going."

A driver has to hook-up and unhook trailers; slide tandems and the fifth-wheel to get the load legally distributed; fix lights, fuses, and connections; load and unload trailers; change fuel filters and adjust brakes; chain and unchain tires during the winter; be patient until it's their turn to load or unload; and keep the inside of their tractor and trailer clean. Ducking under trailers, crawling under axles, climbing in and out of the trailer and on and off of the deck-plate is expected.

Some students are looking for glamour and excitement. Others are running away from something. Still others think it's an easy way to make $30,000 a year. They pay thousands of dollars for their Commercial Driver's License and then try to act the role presented on television and in the movies. By the time they've completed their training on reduced wages, they're either ready to quit or go ahead and be a real driver. Worse yet are the companies who assign them to people not qualified to train them.

Unless the fledgling has a family member or friend to indoctrinate them or the luck-of-the-draw places them with a trainer that teaches them the real responsibilities and rules of being a driver, they'll be burned out and back home owing thousands of dollars for their student loans.

But what happens when the training is good and the student enjoys this mode of earning a living? Beverly has been on big roads, skinny roads, cow paths, and actually drove out into a field to pick up watermelons. She has eaten lobster on both coasts; made angels in the snow by moonlight on Donner Pass; watched rainbows appear and last for miles, seen beauty beyond comprehension, felt humble, and yearned for more. She wouldn't have missed it!

In the '50s and '60s truck drivers would stop to help stranded motorists. Most of them learned to drive from their father, a relative, friend, or in the military. Their truck was a source of income, identity, and pride. They were the equivalent of modern cowboys; worked and played hard, and were respected. Since violence against drivers has become commonplace, they're no longer willing to risk their time, equipment, freight and, in some cases, their life.

When Beverly was a fairly new driver, carrying a load of beer from Houston to Los Angeles, Wendell told her that she wasn't to stop the truck without waking him first. "Even if there's somebody layin' in the middle of the road, you put the peddle ta the metal and make sure they can hear it! If they're dead, it won't hurt 'em. If they're alive, they'll move. Drivers have bin found dead and their cargo gone across here." Needless to say, she never forgot that advice.

That doesn't mean that drivers absolutely won't help the public. Beverly watched a driver holding an accident victim's hand that was pinned in the car by a rod through his leg. There was gas all over that could have ignited at any time, but he didn't leave the man's side until help came and they got him out.

Another time, when a woman drove the wrong way until she hit head-on with another vehicle that killed six people and a dog, the interstate was shut down for hours. Drivers were sharing food, water, and sodas in the blistering heat with 4-wheelers who didn't have anything to eat or drink with them.

Beverly explained to a couple of older women how to urinate into a Zip-Lock bag and let them use her bunk for privacy. By the way, if you happen to see a baggie coming out the window of a semi, duck and wash you car as soon as possible.

When it's below zero, drivers grab the blankets off of their bunks, wrap children in their coats, cry because they can help; more if they can't.

Just as you've seen on television, solo drivers do push themselves past safety limits. It was a continuous reality for Beverly. She drove over-hours in order to get the load delivered on time or be at the shipper in the time allotted by the dispatcher or broker. She gambled her CDL, truck, load, money, as well as her life and the lives of the public. Until technology forces the trucking companies to account for the truck's movement by making company owners pay the over-hour and speeding fines, they'll continue to bully the drivers.

Beverly knows the technology exists to eradicate this practice because she drove for a company who insisted that she drive legally. She was in constant contact with her dispatcher via satellite and was able to type a message to him at any time. This was helpful when the truck broke down in the middle of nowhere or she needed directions. It also gave her a feeling of security when it wasn't safe for her to leave the truck. Now most drivers have cell phones that help with all of these issues.

The American Dream of owning your own truck still lures some inexperienced egos to buy a truck in the belief that they'll be able to pay for it. They buy both the tractor and trailer, buy the tractor and lease a trailer from the company they work for, or buy the tractor and pull a company trailer.

Some companies have lease-purchase plans where a driver is allowed to take charge of a tractor as long as they keep it in good condition and make the payments on time. They pull for only that company. The naive newcomer will find, in most cases, that after maintaining the equipment for most of the leased time, they'll either be required to pay it off in cash as the loads become more scarce, or they'll be asked to renew the lease for updated equipment. Either way, the company maintains control of the equipment, loads, and ultimately the owner operator.

Beverly will drive as a company driver and let the uninformed or extremely wealthy lease or buy trucks. She and Wendell tried a lease/purchase contract with a medium sized trucking company. They ended up spending all of their money on the truck to keep it running, and the company repossessed the truck because they weren't able to pay cash for it at the end of the contract.

Most company drivers are assigned a company tractor. They're responsible for keeping it clean, keeping the shop informed of any problems, and making sure that all pertinent permits are in the truck. They're usually paid by the mile, but sometimes receive an additional amount for pickups, drops, layovers, and lumpers.

Most companies offer life, health, dental and accident insurance. The amount the driver pays differs with the individual company. Some companies also offer 401K plans. Most companies extend cash advances through the driver's fuel card while they're on the road, and most pay for motels during extended layovers.

Being a team means you are partners, will watch each other's back, and do your own share of the work. Most of the time over-the-road drivers deliver in the type of neighborhood that you saw on television during the LA riots, not the safest neighborhoods. These people have nothing. They have nothing to loose by trying to steal what they can from drivers. The only thing that deters them is the knowledge that most drivers carry some type of a weapon and are not afraid to use it.

The basic rules of team driving:

- Learn to back the truck up, otherwise you'll always be second seat and you'll have to wake your partner up every time the truck has to be backed up.
- If you leave the truck while your partner is gone, leave a pillow in the driver's seat. This will notify the other person you have left the truck.
- Respect your partner's bunk hours. Many people like to be left alone to read, do cross-word puzzles, sleep, etc. If they're in the bunk with the curtain closed, don't slam the door or jump on the step as you leave or return to the truck.
- Most drivers will wake up when the truck stops or makes an unusual movement or sound. Don't stop the truck more than is absolutely necessary. Try to drive, shift gears, and break as smoothly as possible.
- You have your partner's life in your hands every time you

take the wheel. Don't take unnecessary chances with your lives and the lives of the public, the truck, the load, or your CDL.

- Never give your partner's logbook to an officer. You're required to show your own, but you don't have to show your partner's.
- Don't use the F-word as a verb. Everyone loses their temper at times, but the abusive language and behavior is frowned on by other drivers, shippers, receivers, dispatch, law enforcement and the public.
- Assess your partner's abilities. If they smoke the brakes going down grades, try to be driving when you get to the grades. If they aren't able to drive past five hours, drive five hours on duty and five hours off duty. Don't put unnecessary stress on them. Your lives and the safety of the equipment, cargo, and the public are at stake. If snow and ice scares them, make it clear to wake you when these conditions are present. If you have sexual encounters with someone besides your partner, go to the other person's truck. This allows your partner to relax in your truck rather than being forced to hang around the truck stop or restaurant.
- Don't allow them to wear spurs. They mess up the floor mats.

Student driver:

They usually aren't paid full wages while they're in training and barely make enough to pay their living expenses on the road. Most companies keep them with a trainer until they've learned the basics of driving, company rules and values, and how to do the paperwork. Not every trainer is qualified. If the student feels they aren't receiving enough or correct information, they're encouraged to ask their safety department for a different trainer. They should be reminded that it's their life and CDL that's at stake. Not to mention the safety of the public.

Beverly was training a young female. They were on their second turn from California. She woke the student up on the west side of Albuquerque. She told her she should get a cup of coffee and take some time to wake up because she'd take over driving on the east side of the city.

"I've got a headache," the student said and rolled over with her back to Beverly.

"Get in the medicine kit and take an aspirin with your coffee." Beverly was unsympathetic. "Headaches, muscle aches, and cramps aren't reasons for this truck to stop. In fact, pneumonia needs documentation to convince dispatch and then they probably won't care! I drove most of last winter with a viral infection I just couldn't shake. Medication kept me on my feet, but I just couldn't get enough rest to get rid of it."

Driver's are replaceable and must perform or loose their income. If the tires weren't turning, Beverly wasn't making money. Students apparently aren't told this as part of their education. Beverly wasn't!

Who were the truck drivers Beverly knew? There were many personalities behind the wheels of those big rigs. They were the gypsies of the 20th century. Most lived trucking 24-7.

Many good drivers left the industry when Commercial Driver's Licenses became mandatory. Some because they couldn't read and were too embarrassed to ask for a verbal examination. Old-timers told Beverly more than once, "Truck driving school graduates are dangerous. They actually believe they can drive a truck after six weeks of training,"

She has to admit that she agrees with them. She never assumes that a truck driver knows what they're doing. When she pulls out into the left lane to pass one, she sits there for a few seconds to make sure the truck is going to stay in the right lane. A new driver automatically turns the wheel to the left when they look in their mirror. It takes practice to stop doing that.

The longer Beverly drove over-the-road, the more she realized just how little she knew right after she graduated from truck driving school and just how dangerous she had been when she first herded that big beautiful blue Kenworth down the interstate. She grew into being a truck driver by experiencing the life of an over-the-road driver. It was an entirely different world on the road. It was similar to living on the streets except she had a dry place to sleep in the bunk; money to buy food, clothes and souvenirs from her trip advances; and no one to watch her back when she was driving solo. That's the reason she carried a weapon with her.

Beverly knew that the people in major cities where she picked up and delivered cargo were armed. She always kept the curtain between the bunk and the cab closed as if there were someone sleeping. Since most companies didn't trust such elite equipment to women by themselves, everyone assumed she had a partner in the bunk. There were even times she would tell someone on the CB, "Daddy's asleep."

Beverly experienced dramaturgical analysis as she slowly found her role and donned the type of costumes to make the impression she chose for herself. She's not sure she consciously made decisions for the props and manners she adopted, but she is pretty sure she chose companies to drive for so she could choose the type of setting.

Truck drivers drive their stage and setting. They can pick the type of status they want to present by choosing which company they drive for and what type of equipment they drive. They also gain status by being a very competent driver, how clean they keep their equipment and themselves, and what attire they choose to wear. They can invent and reinvent themselves, at will, as long as they stay on the road.

Beverly also lived social-exchange analysis. Each person decides how to act from what they may gain from others by doing so. Rather than Beverly driving hammer-down all of the time by herself, she let the macho-drivers take the front and back doors. That way one of them would get caught by police radar and she could keep driving with a clean CDL. It worked very well most of the time.

She knew that many of these drivers thought that she would 'put out' sooner or later if they were nice enough to her. That's what they expected to gain. She knew she probably wouldn't get a speeding ticket. That was her goal. Most of the time they all simply stayed awake through the night by talking on the CB and went their separate ways in the morning.

Some drivers will do things on the road they'd never dream of doing at home. One example that comes to mind is when Beverly first drove solo in a company truck. A couple of owner operators she knew had slowed down to run across Nebraska with her. Drivers coming from the other direction started telling them about one of their company trucks who had lost a set of duals off of his trailer. "We've been trying to get him on the CB but he doesn't answer. He's about five miles ahead of you."

The owner operators told Beverly that they'd catch her at the fuel stop and took off. Before she got to the fuel stop they'd caught him and were bob-tailing back to get his wheels. Come to find out, his wife was in the truck so he had the CB shut off. He didn't want her to hear anything from other drivers that might let her know about his usual habits on the road.

There are also men who would never dream of this type of behavior. Beverly ran with a lot of them. She heard about how wonderful their wife and children were, how much they missed them, and about their dreams of getting off the road and staying home with mama. Here's hoping those dreams all came true. They did for Beverly!

SUPPLIES THAT BEVERLY CARRIED ON THE TRUCK:
Cleaning Supplies:

- Glass cleaner: Clean windows, mirrors, eyeglasses, and gauges.
- Pledge: Clean dash, arm rests, and vinyl on seats, doors, walls and ceiling. Not on the steering wheel, it makes it too slick.
- Carpet Fresh/Febreze: Sprinkle on the carpet before you vacuum and spray the fabrics. Helps make the truck more pleasant to live in.
- 409: Clean the steering wheel.
- Paper towels: Cleaning rags, Kleenex, toilet tissue, after hygiene touch-ups, and Kotex in a pinch.
- DC vacuum: It is imperative to be able to vacuum out the truck.
- Soft hand brush: To sweep out the sand from the floor by the driver's door.

- Hand cleaner/degreaser: Cleans hands and will remove fifth-wheel grease from clothes.
- Detergent/softener/dish soap: It is much cheaper to carry your own. Truck stops have laundry facilities. Use the dish soap on the tandem rails. Grease collects dirt and the soap keeps them clean and easier to move.

First Aid bag:

- Instant Ice packets: These were indispensable in controlling swelling when Beverly broke her finger and when a hose broke and sprayed antifreeze on her face.
- DC heating pad: Used with your preferred balm for sore muscles. It is also nice if your partner tucks you into the bunk with a message.
- Bandages: All sizes of Band-Aids, tape, gauze, salves, ointments and something for burns.
- ACE bandage: Sprains are common, especially for women.
- Vitamins: Beverly carried enough vitamins for a month. They're cheaper to buy at home and you'll need them since you'll have little time to eat in a healthy manner unless you carry your own food.
- Over-the-counter: What ever you usually use for headaches, muscle aches, and colds. It is also a good idea to carry medication for diarrhea and constipation.
- Moisturizers: Lotions, lip balm, and foot moisturizers (*feet need extra care*).
- Deodorants: This includes foot powders.
- Wet-wipes: For hygiene needs between showers. Also wash your face, hands, and feet after driving for hours. (*You and your partner will appreciate you both using these frequently.*)

Clothes:

- Jeans, slacks, shorts, and skirts: Enough for two weeks. If you're out longer, you'll have time to do the laundry at a truck stop.

- Shirts/blouses: Take a variety of tops. You'll be running in all climates. If you take them on hangers, be sure to use plastic so they don't clank and keep the person in the bunk awake. Beverly prefers women's T-shirts. They don't wrinkle while rolled and still look feminine.
- Footwear: Take plenty of socks. Sitting much of the time makes your feet need extra care. Massaging, washing, deodorants, and clean socks will keep your feet in better condition and makes you feel more comfortable. Make sure that you have substantial footwear. Good traction, protection, and support are essential.
- Coats: It's important to carry jackets that you can layer under. In the winter, you'll need coveralls and heavy outerwear. Remember, it snows in the mountains much of the year.
- Miscellaneous: Underwear, sleepwear, and leisure clothes are up to each person's discretion. Keep in mind your partner's right to privacy, respect, and consideration. Beverly prefers silky nightshirts, but she was usually driving with a husband if she wasn't driving solo.

Bedding:

- DC heated mattress pad: It is wonderful when its cold outside or your muscles are sore. It gives you a little extra padding when it's not turned on. It is also much more comfortable while the truck is moving.
- 2 quilts: One goes over the mattress pad; cover up with the other one.
- 2 fleece blankets: Make sure they're both flat (*not fitted*). Mattresses in trucks are odd sizes and you'll find you'll have a more comfortable sleep by using these as sheets. Tuck the bottom one in at the top and sides and the top one in at the bottom and the sides. You can crawl under the top one from the back of the bunk and leave the front tucked in to help hold you in the bunk while the truck is moving.
- Pillows: One or two for the top of the bed to lay your head on

and one king size for each side of you. This will help keep you from rolling around while the truck is moving. Use one pillow to elevate your feet when they are swollen from sitting so much behind the wheel.

Necessities:

- Maps, Atlas, permits, pens, rulers, lighted magnifying glass (*to read smaller maps at night*), CDL, medical card, log book(s), inspection books, etc.
- Shower bag: Keep all of your shampoos, soaps, deodorants, etc. in zip-lock bags inside a large bag to carry to and from the truck stop. Make sure it is large enough to put your clean clothes in for the trip into the truck stop and bring your dirty ones back out.
- Zip-lock freezer bags: Gallon size for women's porta-potties and quart size for men's. New ones can also be used for food storage. The freezer bags are more trustworthy in not leaking and worth a few more cents.
- Plastic grocery store sacks: They hang on the seat armrest and are cheap/convenient garbage bags. They can be reached by the driver and from the bunk. Most stores will give them to you.
- Small plastic baskets: These come in handy to put on the shelves in the bunk for miscellaneous. Otherwise you won't be able to find anything. Nothing stays in place while the truck is moving unless it is secured.
- Plastic tubs to slide under the bunk: Storage is at a premium in a truck. Many new tractors have storage under the bunk that is accessible from inside. Tubs help keep items in order when the truck is in motion.
- Large garbage bags: Use for dirty clothes. They also come in handy to lie on if you have to get under the truck.
- Handheld recorder: It's also a good idea to purchase a recorder with telephone capabilities. Let your dispatcher know that you have it and they'll be less inclined to try to push you past safety requirements of your equipment, road conditions, or your sleep requirements.

- Camera (*disposable*): Beverly carried several. She used them to document traffic accidents and damaged loads. Don't buy an expensive camera. Trucks are broken into all of the time. Don't carry anything that you don't want stolen.

Tools:

- Your trainer will teach you the necessary tools to gather for your own use. Beverly carried a rubber hammer for a tire thumper, a screwdriver with four heads, a wrench to adjust the brakes, pliers, miscellaneous fuses, duct tape, electrical tape, wire connectors, and a thermometer to check the temperature of produce and the reefer.
- Fifth-wheel grease is a real problem to get out of clothes so Beverly used a meat hook to pull the fifth-wheel lever. This also helped her gain leverage. The best way she found to remove fifth-wheel grease from clothes is hand cleaner.

Optional:

- Television: Beverly also carried a VCR. She rented movies when she was laid over.
- Refrigerator: Saves money, time, and is more healthy than eating in greasy restaurants. Eating out is very expensive and you're less likely to over eat if you carry your own food. California has many road-side fruit stands. This not only saves money but helps with constipation which can become a problem from sitting much of the time.
- Thermos and cup: I carried a very large Stanley stainless steel thermos and Stanley, short plastic cup with a cover. The cup was almost as wide as it is tall and sat on the floor of a conventional, between the seats, without tipping over...most of the time.
- Carpet samples: These are lifesavers in front of and between the seats. The larger ones are also nice on the floor of the bunk for warmth. They can be thrown away when they are dirty.

CHAPTER 5

Beverly got hurt in Sparks, Nevada. She was unloading candy and pulled a pallet off the pile then backed into a box of candy. It caught her behind both legs and she went down on the concrete dock with the empty pallet on top of her. After a lot of physical therapy and going back on the road many times, she received worker's compensation for retraining because an MRI showed that she had a bulging disc. She had no idea what she wanted to do with the rest of her life because she had adopted the over-the-road driver role and enjoyed it so much. She felt that she would simply kill some time, heal, and go back on the road, but it didn't work out that way.

Beverly started classes at a community college. She took a lot of foundation courses because, even though she had her GED since she was sixteen, she had not attended very many actual classes in high school. She was forced to quit when she got pregnant in her sophomore year.

Beverly found that she really enjoyed classes. She learned a lot and had much to contribute to class discussions. Her academic advisor was invaluable in helping her find her way through the many choices for classes. She would not have been able to achieve much without her help and support.

Beverly's major was liberal arts until she found sociology and Erving Goffman. She wanted to know how he knew so much about incarceration in prisons and mental hospitals by just working there. She wanted to know how he knew so much about the games she had played in making the impression she wanted by changing the way she dressed, spoke and behaved. She changed her major to sociology and found her niche.

Beverly found her "shrink" in human services class at the community college. It was a three hour evening class. He told the class that they got extra credit for participating in class. At the break of the second class he asked if he could talk to Beverly. He said, "You have all of the extra credit you will ever need. Shut up and let somebody else talk."

Beverly knew that she could trust this man to tell her the truth. After that semester was over, she asked if he would counsel her. He agreed. He worked with her and Viet Nam veterans with PTSD issues. He went to Oklahoma City and counseled after the bombing and she has called him through the years when she wanted to regain her emotional equilibrium. First he helped her find a way to handle her grief at not being able to drive over-the-road any longer. Then he was a great help in her being able to quit getting married all of the time with the belief that she needed a husband to be happy.

As time went on and Beverly became more interested in academia, she decided that she wanted a four year degree rather than a two. She started interviewing possible advisors in four year colleges. The day she met Dr. William was when she really started believing that she might be able to get her undergraduate degree.

Beverly's sociology professor at the community college told her that Dr. William was a nationally quoted sociology and criminal justice authority. He and his wife were also the authorities on the homeless population in Iowa. He said that Dr. William got up every morning to feed the homeless in the city.

Beverly called the university and spoke with Dr. William's wife. She agreed that he was the criminal justice authority at the university and Beverly made an appointment to meet and interview him to see if that was the college she wanted to attend.

The day of the interview Beverly entered his office and introduced herself. She asked him, "Where were you when I needed you?"

He looked puzzled.

She continued, "Well, if you would have fed me when I was homeless, I could still be there waiting for you to feed me instead of sitting here trying to attend classes. I believe in teaching a person to fish, not handing them a fish day after day. When you feed a person, they are stuck by the lake waiting for you to come and take care of them."

The conversation that followed that day made Beverly want this man for her mentor and academic advisor. He urged her to submit a paper to a sociology association and she won an award for her writing. Beverly transferred to the university shortly afterwards.

The population at the university was entirely different than it had been at the community college. Very few people acknowledged Beverly as she met them on the sidewalk or in the class rooms. People had been friendly at the community college. The courses were harder and she floundered for a semester or two. She passed each one, but really struggled. One day Dr. William's wife, her statistics professor, told her, "Maybe you aren't ready."

Beverly knew she was right, but also knew that she would never return if she didn't keep trying. Beverly was scared and definitely out of her comfort zone, but she was also determined to not let herself be defeated. "All they can do is tell me no. They can't kill me."

Dr. William had Beverly contact Dr. Kimberly while she was in her undergraduate classes. Dr. Kimberly was an Assistant Iowa Attorney General. She also had completed her doctorate in criminal justice at a different university.

Beverly was supposed to meet her for an hour that first time, but ended up talking for a long time. Dr. Kimberly urged Beverly to continue her education at the university where she had completed her Ph.D.

Beverly took the GRE test and passed it. She enrolled and was accepted in the master's program in the criminal justice program and moved into student housing the fall semester after she received her undergraduate degree.

Dr. Kimberly became a mentor. Beverly was intimidated at first, but decided to be honest with her about who she was, what she thought, and how she had been affected by the molestation, physical abuse, scapegoating by her family, incarceration in mental hospitals and prison, and the stigma of being an ex-con. They talked about Beverly's concept of *The Steel Ceiling*. It shocked her at times that Dr. Kimberly, as a prosecuting attorney, listened to an ex-criminal. She noticed that Dr. Kimberly nodded her head quite a bit as she spoke and realized later that everything she was telling her was already in books that Dr. Kimberly had read.

Beverly remembers the day that Ted yelled at her, "Why do YOU need a college degree?"

God that statement had hurt her. He had just helped her sister pay to put her oldest daughter through college. Why was she more important? Then Beverly remembered that he hadn't gone very far in school and didn't understand that she couldn't use her body any more to make a living like he did.

Beverly had owned a successful drapery and decorating business, she had been an over-the-road driver, and she was a darned good secretary, but all of those professions were gone because of her back injury and fibromyalgia. She couldn't sit or stand for very long and she certainly couldn't lift heavy bolts of fabric or sit over a sewing machine or typewriter for very long any more.

Beverly doesn't know if he ever understood how important her education was to her. She doubts it. He died before she received her undergraduate degree.

Beverly quit her undergraduate classes several times in order to be there for Ted while he was dying from cancer. The day he told her about his diagnosis, she told him, "I'll back whatever decision you make for yourself." She kept her word. She worked for a temporary service and took him to chemotherapy treatments and other appointments.

Beverly had stayed with Ted years before when he had a stroke and didn't want to be alone at night. She stood on his side when Teddy and Becky wanted to take his driver's license away from him. He finally gave it up when he knew it was time.

On Ted's birthday, Jane and Beverly took lunch and a birthday cake to his house. Jane painted on china and Beverly had asked her to paint two plates for Ted's birthday. One had the house where she had been raised and the other had the beautiful barn that Ted had built.

When Ted opened the present he almost fell off of his chair. His skin turned gray. Beverly caught him and helped him to his recliner. She said, "Jane, call an ambulance."

Ted waved his hand and said, "NO!"

Beverly looked at him and remembered that she had told him that she would back whatever decision he made for himself. She sat down in the other chair and prayed that God would give her the courage to keep her word.

Beverly got up and knelt beside Ted. "Dad, you're in trouble. You're in shock. You are going to die if we don't get you help…I told you that I would back your decisions and I will do that. If you want to die here, I will hold your hand…Is that what you want?"

He didn't say anything and Beverly nodded for Jane to make the call. She did and Ted was taken in an ambulance to the emergency room in the city.

Beverly followed the ambulance. She was scared, but realized that God was in control and that she had done everything she could. She remembered the promise Ann had forced her to make. Ann had insisted, "You have to promise me that if something happens to me, you will take care of Daddy," Beverly promised her.

Beverly's "shrink" calls that promise a caustic promise syndrome. It kept Beverly enmeshed with her father because she didn't want to break her promise to her dead mother. She wanted to keep her word to the woman that she had prayed would die so many years before. When it came to a choice between pleasing her father or her husband, as it always did, she would choose Ted.

Beverly said out loud, "Mom, I kept my word to you. I took care of him when he would let me. I was there for him as much as I could be. Now he's yours!"

After Ted died Beverly continued her education. She interviewed the governor that had presented her with an executive pardon and who was the interim president at the university. She was writing a paper, *The Steel Ceiling*. She wanted to know why he had given her a pardon and not others. What was different about her? He told her that he had considered each case on its own merits. He even gave her a reference letter.

Beverly put together her own session at a professional sociology conference where people with master and doctorate degrees presented their papers for her topic, *Institutionalized Females, Their Barred Opportunities and Resources*. She presented *The Steel Ceiling* paper and didn't tell anyone, except Dr. Kimberly, that she only had a GED. Dr. Kimberly presented a paper in that session and flew to and from Chicago with Beverly. Her support was invaluable because Beverly wasn't quite so scared and intimidated with her in the room.

Beverly also presented her paper, *Over-the-Road Truck Driver from a Female Perspective* to the same sociological association in Minneapolis. She received acclaim from the reviewers and one of them said that he thought she wouldn't tell all of the truth, but he was happy to see that she did. He wondered why she hadn't addressed the pornography that he knew men used on the road. Beverly replied, "Remember, this paper is from a female perspective."

Prior to her graduation for her undergraduate degree, she made her own announcements on the computer. She had them all addressed and sent the ones that didn't include her biological family. She put those on the back seat of her car and left them for several weeks. She just couldn't bring herself to send them.

One day she was talking to Dr. William. She told him that she just knew that her family would make negative remarks about her during the reception that would emotionally hurt her. "They have never had anything positive to say about me."

Dr. William told Beverly that she was not required to invite anyone that she didn't feel comfortable with. Beverly realized he was right and threw the invitations away. She wanted the day to be special. Those people would not be able to help themselves. They would have to find a way to ruin it for her.

Beverly received her undergraduate degree on Mother's Day. She walked across the stage. It was important to her to put on the cap and gown because she had not done so for a high school graduation. It was also important to her because Ann had thought that anyone that went to this particular university was a very intelligent person. Beverly thought to herself as she accepted her diploma, "Hey ma, whatcha think of me now?" She got back to her seat and visualized her dead daughter being proud of her, "I hope you are."

The graduation reception was wonderful. Beverly had borrowed money from an AA brother for a tent and DJ. Her AA brothers and sisters helped her celebrate and Dr. Kimberly showed up, too. She didn't do the chicken dance, but it sure meant a lot to Beverly that she took the time to be there.

Beverly had told Dr. Kimberly to just ignore the crack houses that skirted the property where the reception was held. There were a lot of weeds and trash around the gravel streets. Shortly afterwards, city workers mowed the weeds and the people in the crack houses moved out. Beverly will never know for sure what happened, but she was happy to see them and the excessive traffic leave. Later the main street was blacktopped.

Beverly worked for the Census Bureau that summer and stayed with one of her mentors. She enumerated "the hood" and was chased by big, mean dogs. She figured out to not enter a yard where two large barking dogs are tied up with log chains because there was also another one loose in the yard. She found out that she could still move REAL fast!

Beverly had to ask for a Spanish interpreter because some of the families she found in the alleys of another neighbor didn't speak English. The husband of the female interpreter didn't want her going down the alleys, but Beverly said, "They haven't hurt me and I don't speak their language. I don't want to draw any more attention to them. Let's get this job done."

The interpreter followed Beverly and the people were really nice. Through the interpreter she was able to tell them that all of the information was confidential and would not cause them to be deported. She told them that she had been married to a Chicano from Chicago and they wanted to know why she couldn't speak Spanish. She told them, "He didn't want me to learn because I would know what he was calling me when he was mad."

Beverly moved into student housing at an out of state university to start her graduate classes in criminal justice. Her back was in real bad shape and she pulled her books in a two-wheel cart in the snow, up and down the hill, to and from classes. She had to go outside to smoke, which got pretty darned cold in the winter for someone who had asthma and COPD.

Beverly enjoyed the diversity of her roommates and even met a woman about her same age from Russia. They compared the propaganda they each had each been taught during the cold war.

Beverly struggled to get Bs and was told by a fellow student that he saw no reason for an ex-con to get an education because no one would hire them anyway.

It was always Beverly's goal to work with female prisoners in order to pass on what she had learned. She had promised the Governor that she would do everything she could to make that possible. She knew that she hadn't been socialized to succeed on the outside when she was in prison and the women she met in AA for years were not finding those answers when they were in prison either. She had worked with them, one at a time, for years in AA. She really wanted to make a difference for them; help guide them to better lives. She believed that an education would help facilitate her endeavors.

One evening an international researcher spoke to Beverly's class. She made research sound really interesting and she got Beverly's interest in maybe trying to learn how to do research. After she finished she asked, "Are there any questions?"

Beverly raised her hand. "Where are the statistics from the inmates? What do they have to say?"

She dismissed the question with, "They don't matter."

Beverly's heart was broken. The other student was right. She was wasting her time if human beings didn't matter.

One of Beverly's text books said that over 90% of women in prison had been abused in childhood. What was the difference between children that make national news who are kidnapped and molested and children who endure molestation for years by friends and relatives? Don't they deserve compassion and help finding their way back from terror, depression and self-hatred? Of course, they act out and get into trouble. They self-medicate with alcohol and drugs and try to find someone who will treat them nice. Unfortunately, they usually end up in other abusive relationships.

Beverly ran away when she was young. Wouldn't you run when you are regularly sexually penetrated and beaten? She was too young to fight most of the time.

Beverly had worked hard to fight her way back. She had endured being scapegoated by her biological family, barred from opportunities and resources because of her criminal record, and watched her molester go unpunished.

A psychologist told Beverly that it wasn't cost effective to treat this population. Beverly didn't say anything, but she had watched women she worked with in AA get and stay sober and clean, follow her into academia and become wonderful mothers, sisters, daughters and friends. Maybe Beverly has a different concept of cost-effective.

Beverly went home and prayed. She slept lightly that night because she couldn't get that remark, "They don't matter", out of her mind. How could it be possible that inmates don't matter when she learned that over 90% of female prisoners had been abused as children? Does that mean that she doesn't matter either? After all, she was an inmate for over six years. Of course, she had been on parole for two years and had an executive pardon. That's probably the only reason she was allowed to attend college at all.

Beverly had changed her whole life around. Doesn't that mean that other inmates could change if they were given the opportunity and guidance? Maybe society just needed to get rid of some people when the world economy mandated that third world countries competed for jobs. Maybe society needs somebody to look down on so they can feel better about themselves?

Beverly woke the next morning with the thought, *I don't know who I'm doing this for, but it isn't me!* She went on the web and found the site for the first company she drove truck for. She applied online and received an email that she had a job waiting for her in another state.

Beverly called a woman that she attended AA meetings with. She was Native American, was in undergraduate classes to help her people, and had allowed Beverly to share several sweats with her. Beverly told her that she was leaving and that she could have everything that Beverly would not need on the truck. That included an almost new computer, printer, clothes, etcetera. She and several of her friends helped Beverly empty her room. Beverly drove south to start driving the truck again.

Beverly found the terminal and was partnered as second seat with Lila. She was slender, had short brown hair, and appeared to be an experienced driver.

Their first turn was from Oklahoma City to California and Washington. Beverly ran straight into a whiteout the first time she took the wheel. They were shut down for hours waiting for the blizzard to let up and the highway to be cleared. They delivered in California and slept overnight on the street in Redding because neither of them knew how to put on chains and all of the parking spaces for trucks were filled. Besides, Beverly was taught that it was time to park the truck when chains were required.

They finally dropped the trailer in Washington because they were too late to deliver. Lila got a motel room rather than calling dispatch to find out which trailer they were supposed to grab and run with.

The next morning they were given a trip to Chicago. Lila took the first turn driving. Then Beverly was driving on ice in Idaho. The sign said something about a steep grade for miles. Beverly said, "Oh shit!"

Lila opened the bunk curtain. "Are you okay?"

"Well," Beverly said as she eased the right tires over to the gravel covered shoulder and down shifted, "I think I remember how to do this."

Lila closed the curtain without saying anything. When it opened again Beverly had reached the bottom of the grade and was driving in freezing fog. She could barely see the road past the nose of the tractor, but it was past sun rise so she could see the shadows of vehicles coming at her. Again Lila asked, "Are you okay?"

"So far."

The curtain closed again.

Lila was a great road driver, but couldn't back the trailer into a hole without freaking out. She screamed, yelled, and put the trailer everywhere but where it belonged. She refused to let Beverly try to back it up and found men to help her.

The next trip was supposed to deliver in Salt Lake City. They were in Evanston, Wyoming, several days before the delivery date. It had been a rough few days in the truck with Lila. Following is a portion of Beverly's journal. Lila is trying to back the trailer into a tight parking space:

> Lila had been tense up until that moment, but she came undone. I said that we would have to move the tandems clear back because the "hole" was real tight. She told me to hold the lever so she could move them clear to the front with, "I am NOT moving them back!"
>
> I would whistle when she was about to hit something, two trailers and fence. The more she struggled, the more frustrated she became. Finally a man appeared and told her to move the tandems to the back. She complied immediately. Lila made several more passes at the "hole" and slid over to the "jump seat" when the man offered to park it.
>
> I was not asked if I could hit it. I was simply awakened, told to stand outside and make sure she didn't hit anything. I was frozen by the time the trailer was parked. I climbed into the jump seat and closed the door so I could warm up.
>
> Lila told me to come hold the "pin" out so she could pull the tractor out from under the trailer. I asked, "Can't you hold it while I pull out?" Her sigh of disgust prompted me to climb out of the truck and hold the "pin puller" while she drove forward.

When I got in the truck again she told me that they didn't have a load for us. She bob tailed to a truck stop. We went in the building, had breakfast, and back to the truck. I crawled into my sleeping bag fully clothed, pulled a blanket and my long coat over the top and tried to warm. I hoped that would be enough because Lila didn't turn the heat on. I fell asleep.

I woke to cold feet. The vent by them had cold air blowing full blast. Even pulling them away from the vent didn't help. I climbed out of the top bunk, put on my coat and went into the building. I used the rest room, had breakfast, and called my adopted brother. I went back to the truck and sat in the driver's seat so I didn't bother Lila by moving my bags from the jump seat into the top bunk. Her belongings were in the closet and cabinets. Mine stayed in bags.

After she woke, I threw my bags back on the top bunk and moved to the jump seat. I went into the building with her and drank tea while she had breakfast. At some point she asked me, "Well, do you want to get a room?"

"Not really," I answered, "I can't afford all these motel rooms. I paid for four nights before I got on the truck and half on the one in Washington with you. I told you that I would rather stay in the truck, but you insisted."

She tried to hide her irritation and asked the waitress about a motel close to the truck stop, called and told them she wanted a room. She apologized again for being frustrated the night before and I told her that I understood the frustration, especially when a person is tired. She assured me that she wasn't mad at me…just tired.

She bobtailed to the motel. During the short trip she told me, "We have been fired!"

"What?" I was shocked. I hadn't agreed with most of her actions and decisions, and we had been late for every delivery, but was that enough to fire me?

"Well, I have been fired," she continued. "The broker

doesn't want us to carry their freight any more because we have been late for every delivery." I just sat there looking at her. She continued, "Maybe the owner can put someone else on here with you. The broker doesn't know your name. I've been on the list for a reefer since June anyway." She told me that she would pay for the room as the phone rang.

After she hung up she said, "Well, there goes my motel room, we have to bob tail to Indiana and pick up a trailer."

I tried to hide my pleasure. I wasn't looking forward to another night in a motel room with this woman. She just didn't get it! I didn't want to sleep any place except the truck. I didn't need a baby-sitter.

She bob tailed to Indiana, picked up the trailer and drove to the Flying J at Lebanon. I stood outside while she made a pass at a couple holes. I finally got back into the jump seat. As she was driving back out of the parking lot a driver motioned that he was leaving. I was relieved because it was an easy parking space.

I didn't grab my coat when I got out of the truck because all she had to do was circle, straighten out, and back straight in. I stood in the parking space and watched in horror as the trailer headed in every direction but where I was standing.

After a few minutes she jumped out of the tractor and stomped back toward me. I met her halfway because by this time the trailer was halfway across the lot. She yelled something at me about telling her which way to turn the wheel. I'm sure it made sense to her, but I found it illogical. "Lila," I said, "would you like me to try it?"

"NO!" she screamed. "I'll give it a shot!" She stomped back to the tractor.

The truck moved back and forth in the traffic lanes a few more times, but never came close to the empty parking space. Then she slammed the transmission into a forward gear, swung into a circular motion, came to an abrupt stop, and yelled out the window, "Get in the truck! We're leaving!"

I noticed that my ears were numb as I climbed into the jump seat. Lila was yelling about other drivers talking about her backing up on the CB, "But not one would get out and help me! All you do is stand there!"

Over the CB:

Driver 1, "You aren't going to give up are you?"

Driver 2, "You'll never learn that way!"

Driver 3, "You can't get any easier than that one!"

Lila grabbed the mic. "BITE ME!" She drove out of the truck stop.

I realized how embarrassed she was and how totally inadequate her backing skills were. I said, "We might want to go back one exit. I think I saw some room there. It looked like a fuel stop." When we arrived there was a pull-through parking spot and we were finally settled in for the night.

Lila apologized for being frustrated and repented her anger because the men wouldn't help her. "Its not you!"

I again told her that I understood being frustrated, but wondered to myself what kind of help she wanted, especially with that last hole. We went into the building. I got a donut and chocolate milk and kept my mouth shut. I moved my bags from the upper bunk to the jump seat and again crawled into my sleeping bag…under the blanket and my coat. I fell asleep.

The next morning I woke to cold feet again. Again I got up and went into the building to use the rest room, grab a cup of coffee and warm up. I walked back to the truck and put my bags on the upper bunk. I sat in the jump seat trying to figure out how to deal with this woman. I thought, *Honesty is the best policy!*

Lila woke and asked me, "Are you all right? You are quiet."

"I'm pissed! I'm tired of freezing. I'm tired of your frustration and apologies."

She looked shocked. "You said you understood! I don't think that is fair!"

"Lila," I continued, "I'm not sure I could have hit some of those holes, but I knew I could hit that last one! That's the reason I offered. Last night you discounted me when I mentioned moving the tandems to the back, but a stranger tells you the same thing and you go, 'Oh, all right.' You even let him park our trailer. I would like to be a part of this team!"

She said, "That would be nice!" in a sarcastic voice.

I didn't back off. "And that means?"

She reacted by telling me I was wrong.

"Lila," I was stern, "apologizes don't count if you keep doing the same thing. The third apology isn't going to get it! If you are going to have to say you are sorry, don't do it! And by the way, 'BITE ME!' isn't acceptable. That isn't the image our company wants us to portray."

We were both quiet. She asked me to drive back to the Flying J. I parked the truck and we got separate showers. I called recruiting about becoming a company driver. I didn't want to cause Lila any trouble, but I wasn't going to take much more. I had divorced husbands for less abuse and certainly didn't deserve being yelled at by this woman, especially when all I was doing the first time was sleeping. Hell, the second time I was just standing in a parking spot, doing everything in my power to not laugh at her with the other drivers. I bought a heavy jacket and met her in the cafeteria for breakfast.

During breakfast I said, "I apparently don't know what you call spotting you. All I try to do is make sure you don't hit anything." I don't recall her exact words, but I got the impression she wanted me to tell her when and which way to turn the wheel. I said, "I know how to do that when I am backing up, but I won't even attempt to tell you which way to turn the wheel from outside the truck. How are you going to back it up when there isn't somebody to direct you? There won't always be somebody there. You have to learn to do it yourself and practice is the only way. I had to be willing to look stupid until I didn't have to look stupid anymore."

She wasn't happy about my perspective. She wanted to make it my fault that she couldn't back the trailer into a space. I said, "I'll tell you what. When you see me go into the bunk, you'll know that I've had it."

We got dispatched to LaSalle, Illinois, to give our trailer to another driver and pick up a loaded reefer for Utah. I drove into the truck stop. Lila told me, "I'll go find him," and got out of the tractor. I dropped the trailer in a parking space and asked the other driver for a signed delivery slip. I called Jeff, our dispatcher. I asked him to call Lila on her cell phone. "I don't know where she is. Will you please tell her that the other driver has picked up the trailer?"

I bob tailed to the building and had to yell to get her attention when she walked past me. I moved to the jump seat and logged into the bunk. Lila asked if I had called dispatch. I said, "Yes and I got a delivery slip from the other driver."

She seemed mad, "I'm the one that sent him over there!"

I was quiet. "Now what?" I thought to myself, "She doesn't want me to talk to dispatch? That isn't going to happen. I've had husbands try to isolate me. It didn't work for them either!"

She made phone calls to dispatch. The driver was in the hospital. He owned the tractor that was hooked to the trailer we were supposed to take to Utah. She called the nurse's station for directions to the hospital. I went to the bunk after she turned the wrong way on a one-way street.

She finally stopped in front of the hospital, "You'll have to sit in the seat and move it."

It was my off-duty hours and I was trying to get some rest. I climbed out of the bunk as she was gathering her things. I looked out the side window and saw that she had parked in front of a fire hydrant. I said, "In front of a fire hydrant? I don't think so. I'll go get the keys to his truck and you can get the ticket for being parked here."

I sat back down on the bottom bunk. After some more

discussion, she popped the clutch and I hit my head hard on the top bunk as she put the truck into motion.

I counted to ten REAL slow. She slammed the tractor into the legal parking space I pointed to about a half block from the hospital entrance, climbed to the ground, slammed the door, and went to get the keys from the other driver

I didn't say anything when she came back. Neither did she. She drove back to the truck stop, stopped by the other tractor and handed me the keys. "Drop the trailer and park next to it."

I got our pin-puller out of the side box, dollied the trailer down, unhooked the lines, and pulled the pin. I climbed into the tractor and started it. It rattled and exhaust filled the cab. I turned it off, got out, and told Lila that I was afraid of blowing the motor. She said, "Move it!"

I got back into the tractor and started it again. When the exhaust filled the cab again, I turned it back off.

Let's see, I'm dealing with a person who hasn't demonstrated a great deal of good sense. Also, I was trained to CYA (cover your ass). I asked Lila to let me talk to Jeff, our dispatcher, on the company cell. It was going to be my butt if I blew this man's engine and I wanted Jeff to tell me personally to move it. He told me that I wouldn't hurt, "no longer than you'll have it up."

I went back, started the engine, pulled out from under the reefer and backed it into the spot next to the trailer. Lila gave me a signed delivery slip and the tractor keys for the truck stop manager. They would be held for the hospitalized driver.

I walked from the back of the lot to the building. I wondered if I would ever be able to get warm again. When I got back to the truck she was changing the headlight. I wondered why the tractor was shut off because she had told me that the only times it was shut down was to check the oil or be serviced. The converter that ran the AC television drained the batteries within an hour unless the motor was running.

As usual, it was cold inside the truck and the driver's door was standing wide open. I closed it. She opened it, three times. The fourth time she opened it within a few minutes, I left it open.

I called recruiting on my cell and asked to be taken off the truck as soon as possible. I put on my jacket and covered up with my coat. I lay in the bunk shivering and listening as Lila asked the driver parked in the next spot to fix the headlight. He put it in and jumped our truck to start it. I turned the bunk heat on full blast until I stopped shivering and drifted off to sleep.

I woke as the truck turned off the interstate. We were in Williamsberg, Iowa. I drove to Lincoln, Nebraska, and slowed down for ice from Big Springs, Nebraska, to Cheyenne, Wyoming. I had asked Lila several times why we didn't have a padlock on the load and why the reefer wasn't running since we were supposed to keep the cargo from freezing. All she would tell me was, "I've already talked to Jeff."

During breakfast at Sapp Brothers outside of Cheyenne, she called and told the shop that the reefer battery was dead. After she hung up, she looked at me, "Were you mad at me by the hospital yesterday?"

"Yes," I said, "and I was pissed back at the truck stop. You turned off the truck and left the door wide open."

"Why didn't you just shut it?"

"I did! Three times! When you opened it the forth time I called recruiting and asked to be taken off of the truck as soon as possible."

"I don't think that is fair," she whined.

"Lila, I'm not going to freeze in and out of the truck!"

After breakfast the shop got the reefer running so the cargo would not freeze going over the mountains and serviced the tractor motor. As usual, we were late delivering. We were supposed to be in Salt Lake City by 4:00 PM on Friday and the receivers weren't open over the weekend.

Lila asked, "Do you want to get a room?"

I had already told her that I couldn't afford it. Since that didn't work I said, "Look, I used to have a high sex drive. Now that I'm 56, it's better, but I have a vibrator and eight new batteries. I would like some space to use them! Please! Get your motel room and allow me time in the truck by myself."

She didn't say anything. Guess there wasn't anything to say. I went to the bunk for a nap and she drove.

In Evanston, Wyoming, she told me after I woke up at the Flying J Truck Stop, that dispatch had authorized her to get a motel room and me to stay in the truck, "Will you drive me over to the motel? We will leave about 7:00 AM on Sunday. Call me for sure then."

"Sure." I was relieved. She tried to get me to go the wrong way on a one-way street. I ignored her and went to the interstate, made a U-turn at the next exit, and dropped her off at the motel.

I drove to the Pilot Fuel Stop because I thought it would be a quieter parking lot than the Flying J and it was within sight of the motel where Lila was staying. I backed into a parking space where I could see the entire lot. I called Lila to tell her where I was parked in case she wanted to get something out of the truck. I left a message for our dispatcher, telling him where I was parked, what motel Lila was in, and my cell number. I turned on there stereo, light jazz, and settled in for a non-traumatic evening.

God, it was wonderful. There was heat in the bunk and I didn't wake with cold feet. I got up the next morning, drove to the fuel island to fuel the reefer, and backed into the same space.

While I was paying for the fuel, I bought Windex and

> paper towels so I could clean the windows and mirrors. I had shown Diane that the bolt holding the weight on the driver's side step mud flap was missing, but she had been unconcerned. I looked in the store for a replacement, but ended up taking the weight off and putting it in the side box so it didn't fall off and injure a motorist.
>
> The next morning I got up at 7:00 AM and waited for Lila's call to pick her up. I waited until almost 10:00 AM to call her. She acted like she couldn't hear me by saying, "Hello?" over and over.
>
> I called dispatch to see if my phone was working. She could hear me fine. I explained the situation. The dispatcher called me back and told me that she didn't know what was going on, but Lila wasn't answering the company cell. She had put it on voice mail. Dispatch told me, "Drive to the motel and find out ."

Beverly never found out what was wrong with Lila. All she knew is that the motel management and maids were worried about her behavior. They said that even the person that delivered pizza to her room had conveyed concern about her being naked with the sheets and blankets on the floor instead of on the bed. Lila was almost incoherent with slurred speech when the manager tried to let Beverly into the room. Lila held the door open only a couple of inches, but wouldn't let her in. She told Beverly that she'd be down in a few minutes, but she didn't show. Dispatch sent Beverly on to Salt Lake City with the load.

Beverly delivered the load on time the next morning in Salt Lake City and dead-headed into Idaho to pick up the next load. Dispatch said to pick up Lila in Evanston on her way to Oklahoma City. Beverly asked if Lila was going to be safe to ride with and was assured that she had been told in no uncertain terms to behave. Things were a bit tense on the trip back to the terminal, but much less than it had been prior to whatever happened to Lila in the motel.

Apparently dispatch noticed that Beverly delivered and picked up on time when she was in the truck by herself. She was assigned a beautiful owner-operator's Freightliner pulling a reefer. It was great having a truck all to herself again. Problem is, Beverly was 56. She simply didn't have the energy she had when she was in her 40s and she asked to sleep more than she had the last time she worked for that company.

One evening after Beverly delivered in San Antonio, a man tried to rape her. She had showered, eaten in the truck stop restaurant, and was walking back to her truck that was parked next to the open shop bays. A man walking a couple steps behind her asked how she was doing. She said, "Good." As she started to turn toward the driver's side of her tractor, he grabbed her left arm and drug her toward the door. She put her keys back into her right pocket, doubled up her fist, and swung with everything she had. It didn't even faze him. She started laughing. Her thought was, *This is a hell of a time to find out that I don't have any strength left!*

The man looked startled at her laughter. Then she started yelling at the people in the open shop doors, "Call the police! RAPE! RAPE! RAPE!"

The men in the shop started running in her direction while others grabbed their cell phones. The man let go of Beverly's arm and ran down the side of the trailer and out of sight. Her saviors asked if she was all right and she thanked them for their efforts. She climbed into her truck and locked the doors. She called dispatch on her cell. She told them what had just happened and asked to bounce back to the terminal for some time off to go home. They agreed.

Beverly drove to Oklahoma City, got into her car and drove home. A few days later she called recruiting and asked if there was anyone, other than Lila, that she could team with. An owner-operator was interested in teaming with her.

This one was even worse! He had only one bunk in the truck and one of them had to sleep on the floor in front of the bunk or across the front seats. At first he told Beverly that her smoking didn't bother him, but as time went on he nagged her more and more about it. She didn't shift gears to please him, accelerate or break the way he wanted her to. She didn't drive fast enough or far enough for him. She parked in the wrong truck stops. You name it.

There was a gauge behind the bunk that was supposed to tell him how to load the trailer so it was legal. The last trip Beverly drove with him, he got into the trailer and rearranged the cargo and told her to drive over the DOT scale. It cost him around $300 for that overweight ticket. He also had to get back into the trailer and put the cargo back the way it was.

Beverly got off that truck when they returned to terminal, put her belongings in her car and drove home. She used the excuse that she wanted to change companies so she could get home more often, but realized that she would rather deal with the prospect of being harmed once in a while driving solo than the constant tension of driving team.

Beverly called a trucking company about one hundred miles from her home. She was hired, went through orientation, and was assigned a tractor pulling 53 vans. She drove solo and was routed mostly east with this company. Of course, being a west coast driver, she was not as comfortable because she didn't know every hill, curve, etc. After three months she was fired for too many late deliveries. She was devastated because she had given driving everything she had. She realized that she was getting older and simply did not have the energy to keep up anymore.

Beverly contacted another small trucking company a few miles further away. She was assigned a tractor and drove solo for a while. She got pneumonia and the doctor told her to go to bed. She faxed the slip from the doctor to the company.

Beverly was in bed asleep on 911 when her roommate told her to turn on her television. She laid there and watched the planes hit the towers over and over again for what seems like weeks. She was emotionally traumatized over and over again when she saw people jumping to their deaths, but couldn't seem to turn the TV off because, along with the rest of the country, didn't know what was going to happen next.

The day before Beverly went back out on the road, she called the FBI and left a message. "I know you probably have already thought about it, but I need to tell you that people from that part of the world have been learning to drive semi just like those pilots that hit the towers. When I think about the devastation that a small truck caused in Oklahoma City, it scares me what a semi full of chemicals could do. I have watched quite a few drivers get out of their truck, get down on their rug and pray in the truck stops. I know it is illegal for you to profile, but know that I will be profiling and scrutinizing the drivers around me."

Beverly started driving truck again the next morning. She noticed that the drivers that had been wearing turbans were no longer wearing them. Neither were there any togas. Jeans and cowboy shirts were the apparel now.

Beverly lost a filling and asked dispatch to go home to have it replaced. She told them that she had a toothache. They didn't care and sent her south. When she returned home a few days later, she stopped by the house and dumped her belongings. A friend followed her to the terminal where she left the tractor. She came home. She thought it was for the last time.

Beverly finally made the decision to stay home and find a job. She realized that she no longer fit into the world of over-the-road truck driving. She was fifty six and didn't have the energy to work twenty four to thirty hours without sleep. She was afraid that she would fall asleep behind the wheel and hurt someone. It was either getting more dangerous for a woman to drive solo or she was not willing to take that risk any more, probably a little of both.

Beverly was devastated for a while. She had failed in graduate classes and now as an over-the-road semi driver. She applied for and received unemployment. She settled into her rented room and started sending out resumes.

Finally, Beverly was hired as an investigator by a non-profit advocacy agency. She worked there for a little over a year. She was ecstatic because her salary was over thirty thousand dollars a year and she was able to investigate alleged neglect and abuse of people with disabilities. She was able to help people locked on psychiatric wards where she had been housed decades before. Reading their medical records proved to her that childhood sexual abuse had contributed to their dysfunctional lives. Most were not receiving post traumatic stress disorder (PTSD) treatment and many of them were being sent back to live with their abusers. No wonder they were not able to find their way into productive lives.

In the beginning, the staff worked together. They went outside and talked during their smoke breaks. Then, one by one, the smokers resigned. After the manager's son was hit by a car and later died, Beverly was also terminated. Beverly said that she was fired and the manager said that she quit. Beverly took the case to the Iowa Supreme Court, but lost. She knows in her heart that she did the right things and gave the job her best effort. Her conscience is clear and she can live inside her own skin! What a gift.

Beverly worked for a federally funded elderly program where she received minimum wage and could not work over twenty hours a week. That paid her rent, but did nothing for other living expenses. She couldn't even afford a bus pass, let alone food. She quit that job and started vacuuming parking lots with a testosteroned vacuum on a dump pickup truck. Men from a criminal justice halfway house picked up litter from sidewalks and medians. Beverly vacuumed the sand left over from winter and litter on the paving. It still amazes her how many feces filled diapers, used condoms and other obnoxious items are left in parking lots.

Beverly was hit again by a drunk driver. The first one, three years before, injured her back, neck and shoulders. This one gave her a traumatic brain injury (TBI). She went to court the day he was arraigned, introduced herself, "You hit me!", and shook his hand. She wanted him to feel her skin, look her in the eyes and realize that there was a human being in that metal coffin with wheels that he hit. She doesn't know if it made any impression on him, but it helped her find some peace.

At first Beverly didn't know what was happing. She had to ask everyone to slow down when they were speaking to her so she could understand them. Then one of her friends was talking to her and everything was garbled. At first she thought he was kidding, but soon realized that no human voice could make that sound on purpose. She cried for a while and later she could understand English again, but still had to ask that everyone speak very slowly. When she told Dr. Kimberly about it, she said that Beverly needed to see a doctor because something was wrong.

Beverly saw the doctor and was diagnosed, after a lot of

procedures, with post concussion syndrome. This started her journey back from total confusion. She continued to vacuum parking lots, but noticed that she stopped at green lights. People in other vehicles honked at her and called her nasty names. Today she doesn't blame them. She probably scared the hell out of them. But at the time, she simply looked at them. She didn't understand that she had done anything wrong. Her brain registered a traffic light and that she should stop, no matter what color it was.

One night Beverly was stung by a wasp while she was vacuuming. She ended up in an ambulance to the hospital with pneumonia with more confusion. More feeling out of control and lost. She had to start wearing a dust mask when she vacuumed because of her COPD.

Beverly started playing spider solitaire on her computer to help her regain some semblance of focus and reasoning. She remembered that she had heard somewhere that the brain would rewire itself after injury. The pains on top of her head were excruciating. They were on each side of the top. The left was longer than the right, but the same in intensity. She played the game through the pain. She was determined to not let herself give up. She didn't know where she would end up, but she knew that she didn't want to end up like the person that she had investigated with a TBI when she worked for the advocacy agency. She was real careful to keep herself under emotional control. No one was going to lock her up again if she had anything to do with it!

What actually happened is that Beverly felt nicer than she did before the injury, happier most of the time. There were certainly periods of depression, but they weren't the depths of the abyss she had lived with most of her life. Later, she learned that everyone has some type of personality change with a traumatic brain injury. Today she is happy that hers was a positive personality change.

There was a lot of paperwork to do for Beverly's attorney concerning her claim against the drunk driver's insurance company. She couldn't believe how long it took her or how hard it was to remember different words that she had once been able to spout with no effort. Once, it took her over twenty four hours to remember the word "generalize."

Finally, Beverly remembered that there was a TBI organization. She remembered a speaker from that organization when she worked at the advocacy agency. Neither her doctor, nor her attorney had told her about them. She contacted the organization and was sent a tote bag with a video and information about brain injuries. She also got a tote bag for her doctor and attorney. She asked both to pass on the information to others with TBI so they didn't have to flounder in confusion like she had been doing.

The insurance company bought Beverly's car and then sold it back to her for a reasonable price. Little did she realize that the frame had been bent. She drove that poor car over two years until a mechanic refused to fix it because it was "not road worthy."

Beverly received a small settlement from the accident that helped her survive for a short time, but eventually she had to take another over-the-road driving job. This time it was with an owner-operator from a neighboring town. She was insulted when he asked her to drive a truck with an automatic transmission. She thought he had given her "a girl truck." After all, she had driven transmissions from eight to fifteen gears over the years. Later, in Chicago rush-hour traffic, she decided that she never wanted to go back to standard transmissions. Her legs were not cramping from using the clutch all of the time and she eased along without effort.

The major problem Beverly had this time on the road was that her mind wouldn't keep up with what was going past or in front of her when she drove over 60 miles per hour. She recognized that she was a hazard and it scared her. She still had the tendency to stop at green lights and had to really concentrate in order to recognize the difference of green and red to respond appropriately. She could see the correct colors, but her mind didn't seem to know what to do with the information.

After a few turns with no change in this dangerous impediment, she once again got off the road. This time she was sure that she would never drive semi again. She told herself that she was too old and didn't have the energy anymore. "Let the youngsters do the hard work."

Beverly drove over-the-road for over six years all together. The only damage she did to anything was ripping the mud flap on driver's step off one night when she hit a skunk and another night she hit an alligator (truck tire tread) on the interstate which broke the weld on the same step, both in Nebraska. She is extremely grateful for that safety record and doesn't feel the need to push anyone's luck farther by trying to drive semi again.

Beverly received unemployment again for a while. She sent out a lot of resumes. There were always a lot of people applying for the same jobs and most had more education and experience. She volunteered to help in a state agency and was hired as a legal secretary.

One morning Beverly's landlord, the person she considered to be her adopted brother, started yelling at her in the common area of the house. He was mad that she didn't want to clean the common areas and do the dishes for a week at a time. That had not been the understanding they had when she moved in and her back and shoulders wouldn't take swinging the large mop he used. He told Beverly that each person that rented a room would take their turn. She asked why, since they were all adults, they couldn't clean up our own messes. He wouldn't listen. She remembers the fear she felt as he became louder and louder.

He was so loud that her roommate upstairs could understand everything he said and told her later that she should contact the police about being verbally intimidated and abused.

Beverly went upstairs and contacted her vocational rehabilitation counselor and one of her mentors to ask for help in moving. She found an apartment right away. Her mentor helped her pay the rent and deposit. She went home and told her landlord that she was moving and would pack her things. The next morning he started yelling again and called her a conniving, sneaky bitch. He went to his room and slammed the door.

Beverly was in shock at his behavior. She knocked on his door and told him that he didn't act that way when another woman moved out. She didn't see him again until after she moved. She invited him for dinner and cards. He acted like nothing had happened. She still doesn't know what it was all about, but understands that it was his deal, not hers.

Beverly gave it her all when she worked for the state agency, but there is a lot more that she would need to learn before she could be considered a legal secretary. She was offered the opportunity to quit, but told her supervisor that she would prefer that she be fired so she could get unemployment. She had no other means of support and had just moved to an apartment with more obligations. Her supervisor fired her and sent her vocational rehabilitation counselor a very nice letter of recommendation. She will always be grateful for her kindness.

After sending out a lot more resumes and not gaining any type of employment, she finally applied for Social Security disability. There were many tests and much information requested. She dutifully complied and kept playing spider solitaire. By this time the pains on the top of her head were minimal. She had started being able to understand others at almost a normal conversation speed. Her vocabulary was increasing significantly, but her brain still glitched like a computer that can't quite come up with the correct information. She learned to wait and most of the time the words or thoughts materialize.

Beverly started receiving SSDI and asked her vocational rehabilitation counselor to have her cognitively tested to see if she was capable of doing graduate work because she wanted to apply for a grant to attend graduate classes in vocational rehabilitation counseling at a local university. She was tested and it was decided that she could perform in an acceptable fashion with very few accommodations. She applied for the grant and was accepted. She assigned her Ticket to Work and started classes. She was asked to join The National Scholars Honor Society.

She considers herself to be a miracle to have survived all of the negative things that have happened to her and so very blessed that she is able to attend such a prestigious university. So many people never recover from being molested and beaten in childhood; having their family scapegoat them; incarceration in mental hospitals and prison; rape; alcoholism and drug addiction; and traumatic brain injury. Let alone have the opportunity to gain an education to help others.

Beverly found a wonderful friend to share her hopes, dreams, successes and disappointments with. She found herself learning to truly appreciate another person for who he is. She has never known another man that was as sensitive and kind to her as he was. She ended up adoring him. He moved into the apartment. That certainly helped with living expenses and helped her feel more secure in a neighborhood that is known for lots of drugs and parties, but his real gift to her was helping her take responsibility for her own feelings and be accountable for her own behavior.

She learned to stop when she wanted to be mean, go into a room by herself, and take her own inventory. She looked not at what he had done, but what her reaction was to what he had done. What was there from her past that made her scared? That's usually what makes her angry: fear. She found that she was becoming the person she always wanted to be. She can now look at herself realistically and understand that the past, many times, controls her reactions today.

Beverly's life got better when she realized that her life is simply a series of AFGOs (Another Freaking Growth Opportunity). There is always something to learn in every situation, good or bad. When she stopped feeling like a victim and realized that she was living an adventure, she started living a more productive life. When she realized that gratitude and a positive attitude drew good things to her and depression and a bad demeanor drew bad things to her, she had a reason to maintain a confident stance.

She believes that her Higher Power is guiding her to fulfill her destiny. All she has to do is continue to do the next right thing and all will be well. What a blessing!

There are times when Beverly still wonders, *It is all right to be who I am. I have earned the right to exist. I wonder why I had to earn that right. Wasn't I worthy when I was born?*

Beverly hopes that other women living with the after effects of childhood abuse will learn to re-frame their experiences and place the blame where it belongs: on the sexual predator. She hopes they will not recreate their childhood by continuing offensive behavior toward their own children. She hopes that society will finally start making people pay appropriately for ruining lives, especially if the betrayal is from family, friends and acquaintances. She hopes that yesterday's sexual victims, who have ended up in mental facilities and prison, find a positive way to live. Restorative justice gives them the right to finally find solace.

Beverly hopes that congress will make and enforce laws that have zero tolerance for the exploitation of children and insist that predators are punished for the long-lasting effects of their victimizations.

The book Ms. Kern is writing now is called *The Steel Ceiling*. It extends the paper she presented to the Midwest Sociological Society in 2000, with the same title, as an undergraduate student and addresses the internalized, social and political barriers women in the Iowa criminal justice system face in trying to obtain dignity and independence. From necessity, she will compare the rehabilitation criminal justice model of the 1960s and 1970s to the punitive, restorative justice and drug culture models of the present.

Printed in the United States
97455LV00001B/105/A

9 781424 172108